PIRATES
OF THE
IMPERIUM

MARK O'BANNON

Published by MEOw Publishing.

Visit our website at: www.MEOwPublishing.com

First published in 2024

ISBN 978-1-933888-42-2

Printed in the United States of America

This book is dedicated to my friend,

Gigi Edgley

CONTENTS

Go To:
www.MEOwPublishing.com
to see a high quality map of the Imperium

"Who, if I cried out, would hear me among the angels' hierarchies? And even if one of them suddenly pressed me against his heart, I would perish in the embrace of his stronger existence. For beauty is nothing but the beginning of terror which we are barely able to endure and are awed because it serenely disdains to annihilate us. Each single angel is terrifying. And so I force myself, swallow and hold back the surging call of my dark sobbing. Oh, to whom can we turn for help?"

— Rainer Maria Rilke

CHAPTER ONE
Crystalline Wine

3234 A.D. — YEAR OF THE WOOD TIGER

AZURE DRAGON OF THE EAST

HD 172051 / BIJON BLEU

The immense sphere of brilliant energy scintillated in the darkness. A radiant purple ring of fire swept out from it's core, searing a hole in the cold. The starship emerged from the whirlwind, sliding through the night. The sphere of light gradually faded into the maze of stars, like a hot coal burning out of existence. Painted on the hull, next to the Imperial Star, was the name of the starship, the *Ha Ni He*. Propelled on solar sails, it sailed towards the planet, Bijon Bleu.

Captain Sean Greer walked over the main deck of the *Ha Ni*

He, surveying his crew with a practiced eye. On a small viewer he watched Starsinger Talia Bousset inside the cathedral chamber housing the solar sails. Talia closed her eyes in concentration while she focused on the celestial spirit inside the star, HD 172051. She sang a beautiful melody, and tuned the solar sails to match the light frequency of the star. He heard Sailing Master Alonso Moretti call out a command on the intercom, "Retract the hypersails and extend the solar sails."

Greer retrieved a pocket watch and glanced at it, hoping they'd arrive on time. He looked up through the transparent hull overhead at Bijon Bleu, a drop of water in an ocean of darkness. Silver moonlight from the two moons fell onto the night side of the planet. He saw the hypersails retract into the cathedral chamber and watched as the solar sails were extended beyond the transparent force field into space. Star riggers climbed into tubes within the nine masts of the starship, which led upward into the web of solar sails. Greer heard approaching footsteps and dropped his eyes to see Lieutenant Wilhelm Binner. "Sir, we've just detected a corsair on an approach vector."

"How fast are they traveling?"

Binner handed a spyglass to the captain. "A hundred kilometers per second."

Greer opened the electronic spyglass and peered at their pursuer through the energy barrier covering the star deck. The corsair was just a tiny pinpoint of light to their aft. "Not as fast as us," he said.

Binner nodded. "Strange though."

"What?"

"They're decelerating."

"Indeed?" Greer closed the spyglass and handed it back to Binner. "How did it get inside the security perimeter?"

"It's an advanced military stealth ship."

"So it's one of ours?" asked Greer.

"No, sir," said Binner. "It is, however, broadcasting an unusual identity beacon."

Binner handed a computer tablet to Greer. The tablet displayed a hologram of a skull with crossed swords underneath, next to a champagne bottle. Greer shook his head and muttered, "Hosits humani generis."

"Excuse me, sir?"

"It's an ancient Latin phrase," said Greer. "Enemies of the human race."

Binner gritted his teeth. "Aliens."

Shaking his head, Greer handed the tablet back to Binner. "No, lieutenant. They're pirates. Fortunately, we're moving too fast for them. Remain at full sails for the time being. Better man the guns, though, just in case. Load the blaster canons with roundshot.

Sound general quarters."

"Aye, aye, sir."

Binner activated the intercom and blew a whistle to get the crew's attention. "General quarters. General quarters. All hands, man your battle stations."

Throughout the starship, crewmen dropped what they were doing and rushed to report to their duty stations. Airlocks were closed. Warbots took up stations outside the star deck and engineering. The gun decks were cleared of equipment by robot slaves. Pulse laser canons were activated and the blaster canons were primed with energized atomic particles.

*   *   *

As the *Ha Ni He* glided through space on an approach to the planet Bijon Bleu, gun ports along it's side opened up, revealing a broadside of pulse lasers and blaster canons. Far behind the *Ha Ni He*, their pursuer caught a glimmer of starlight on its black hull.

A soft woman's voice spoke calmly over a communication channel, "Graviton device initiated. Five, four, three, two, one, mark."

A silent flash erupted to the side of the *Ha Ni He* and the starship lurched to a sudden halt, immobilized. The sleek corsair, painted black, was upon it's prey. Firing it's guns, the corsair scored a hit and punched holes in the solar sails. The *Ha Ni He* returned fire, shooting it's pulse laser cannons and blasters into the darkness, missing. The corsair fired again, shearing off the masts completely. With wrecked masts hanging over the main deck and the rest of the rigging in a tangled mess, the *Ha Ni He* was completely helpless. The corsair approached and fired grappling lines.

Two dozen figures with personal force fields emerged from the corsair, jumping across the distance between the two starships. Just as they reached the *Ha Ni He*, their shields glowed red. Striking the hull, they burned right through it. As they passed through the hull of the *Ha Ni He*, the breaches were filled with small energy fields that held off the vacuum of space.

The long, sterile corridor gleamed under a harsh white light. Red-hot rings flared on the bulkhead as the assault team's personal force fields seared through the starship's hull. A quick pulse of blue energy sealed each hole, leaving the breaches covered in shimmering, static barriers.

The pirate boarding party stepped into the passageway. All wore black, skintight pressurized space suits. They carried laser pistols and blasters. With a touch, their helmets vanished into a pocket dimension.

Captain Seraphine DeVere was a woman with an air of quiet superiority. Her long dark hair was carelessly tied up into a ponytail. Her cold blue eyes were storm clouds on the horizon, ominous and brooding. But if you looked hard enough, there was a flicker of something else there, too. Beneath the gathering storm, there lingered a spark of wonder, as though the mysteries of the universe still whispered to her in the calm before the tempest. She pulled her laser pistol from its holster, checked the charge—full, as expected—and set it to stun.

Christian Thiessen, the quartermaster, flanked her on the right. His face was grim and his eyes were clear, like a man who had seen too much to be surprised by anything. His movements were measured, efficient, without room for hesitation or sentiment. On the left was Gisela Ellestad, the Starsinger, with her blonde hair falling in waves—pretty, in a way that didn't belong in a place like this. Over her sleek space suit, she had tied a bright, fluttering scarf around her waist. Around her ankles, soft bells chimed in a quiet, tinkling melody—like the distant laughter of some mischevious spirit.

The rest of the boarding party filed into the passageway, swiftly taking up their assigned positions, weapons at the ready. Sentinel 12, the warbot, powered up with a low hum. Its electromagnetic coil gun deployed with a precise, mechanical click, its targeting systems locking on to the corridors ahead.

Seraphine noticed that the passageway wasn't cold. *Heat and light*, she thought. *How delightful.* Her lips curled into an amused smile. She glanced at the others, savoring the inevitable moment of realization that would follow. *Let the games begin*, she mused.

Christian looked at a hand scanner. "Gravity and atmosphere. Bloody hell!"

Lucius, one of the other crewmen, shot a look at the healer, Claude Galen. "So we have a crew to deal with."

Seraphine tilted her head, keeping her tone as cold as a blade's edge. "They're only provincials," she said. "Take care of 'em, Christian. Remember, no lethal force is to be used unless it is absolutely necessary."

Christian raised an eyebrow, his surprise evident. "You don't want me to kill anyone?"

She smirked, her gaze never leaving him. "No. We're not animals." Her voice dropped a shade lower. "But we can still have fun, can't we?"

Christian tucked his hand scanner away. "If this were an unmanned starship, all we'd have to do is sever the guidance beacon from the computer and replace it with ours. Redirect the starship to a pickup spot and unload the cargo."

Seraphine wanted to tell him to shut up, but resisted the impulse. Families always had their squabbles, and he was part of her adopted family, just like the rest of the crew of her starship, the *Lethe*.

He continued, "No, you had to attack a —"

"Mr. Thiessen," Seraphine cut in.

He interrupted her back, "You've never seen a man hanged aboard ship, or tossed out an airlock, have you, captain?"

Seraphine shook her head. "Nothing is more precious than a human life."

"This is a precious sorry business," he grumbled. "Precious is what I'm talking about. My life, and yours," He glanced at the others, "and their lives, too."

"As I told you, Mr. Thiessen," she said. "No unnecessary killing." Seraphine always used his last name when she wanted him to hear what she had to say.

Christian sighed theatrically, as though the weight of the universe rested upon his shoulders. "Very well, captain. I swear by the blood in my heart." He drew his laser rifle with a flourish. "I promise to be gentle."

Seraphine couldn't help but feel the tug of amusement at his defiance. *Why is he always fighting me?* It was a dance they had performed countless times, but the rhythm never lost its thrill. A long, drawn-out sigh escaped her lips. "Just follow my orders."

A few of the others muttered under their breath. Christian turned to glare at them. "Hold fast. You'll obey orders from your captain or I'll strand you on an asteroid you mutinous rogues."

Seraphine held back a grin. Christian, always the blunt instru-

8

ment, had a way of making things fun.

Christian winked at her. "I will look to it, captain."

Her tone was both a command and a subtle invitation for trouble. "Good."

Out of the corner of her eye, Seraphine saw Gisela smiling at Christian. Sela's voice, soft and gentle, was the same heard over the communication channel. "You can't help yourself, can you?"

Christian shook his head. "There's none that can save the captain from herself, missy, but I can try."

The heavy footsteps of a robot slave echoed down the passageway, its mechanical frame casting a long shadow in the dim light. It came to a halt in front of the intruders. Its photoreceptors flared to life with a soft blue glow, scanning each of them with unnerving precision. The machine was obviously built for menial labor. Its design had been stripped down to the essentials for functionality. Its eyes fixed on the pirates with cold, calculating intent.

Sentinel 12, positioned just behind Seraphine, swiveled its weapon with mechanical precision. The electromagnetic coil gun hummed to life, its targeting system locking onto the robot's chassis. In an instant, the coil discharged, sending a high-density polymer projectile directly into the robot's central processing unit. The projectile was designed to deliver high energy to targets inside a starship while dispersing the kinetic force in a way that prevented hull penetration. It transmitted a deadly shock wave without high penetration. A crackling explosion of sparks erupted from the robot's core, and the machine's body jerked violently before crumpling to the floor in a heap of smoking metal. Its eyes flickered one last time before going dark.

Seraphine's eyes glinted as the last sparks from the robot fizzled out. She tilted her head , watching the smoke rise from the wreckage with a hint of amusement. *I'm starting to enjoy this*, she thought. Her voice was light, almost cheerful. "Right. I'll nick the sunstones."

Without waiting for a response, she motioned to her chief engineer, Jorge Segura, and they both strode off down the passageway. The faintest chuckle escaped her lips, the kind that promised trouble.

*   *   *

The crew of the *Ha Ni He* had fallen onto the floor of the command deck when the starship had lurched to a stop. One by one, they got up and returned to their stations. Greer peered at a cracked display showing the damage to his starship. Lieutenant Binner examined it, too. "Looks like we struck a gravity mine, sir."

Greer noticed a breach in the hull, displayed on the console. "Give me an internal view."

The image changed to show Gisele standing by the warbot, Sentinel 12. Gisele sang to herself a beautiful melody. Noticing the camera, Gisele turned to look directly at it and smiled. She touched a device and the display scrambled to static.

Greer frowned. "Alert the crew. We have intruders. Send out a distress signal. Perhaps there is a patrol ship near Bijon Bleu."

Lieutenant Binner nodded. "Aye, aye, sir."

*　*　*

Seraphine and Jorge Segura walked down a passageway and came to the entrance to the energy matrix chamber, where several crewmen worked at consoles, along with a few robot slaves. Jorge drew his laser pistol and took aim. Seraphine put her hand out and waved him to lower his weapon. "Your weapon isn't set to stun," she whispered.

Irritated, Jorge looked down at his laser pistol and changed the setting to stun, just as a pulse of laser light struck the wall to his side. Jorge ducked out of the way while Seraphine drew her laser pistol, took aim and shot three times, striking all of the crewmen. The robots ran frantically away down another exit.

Inside, the tall gallery was filled with lavender light. Three meters tall and suspended in a stream of energy, a giant sunstone hovered. Jorge examined a hand scanner while Seraphine took a moment to admire the giant crystal. "Imagine, just one sunstone is enough to power an entire starship," she whispered.

Jorge smiled. "I've located the vault, captain."

11

Christian, Lucius, Galen and the rest of the boarding party moved down a passageway and stopped at an intersection. An imperial crewman stood in the open, his hands in the air. "Don't shoot! I'm unarmed."

Christian and Galen stepped out into the open. Christian motioned for the man to lay down on the deck. Instead, he smiled. An imperial soldier stepped out of hiding and shot a disintegrator rifle. The beam of light streaked down the passageway and lit up Galen's force field. A half second later, the shield collapsed and Galen was killed as the atoms of his body were scattered into the air, dissipating into nothingness. Christian retreated around a corner. He leaned against a wall and closed his eyes. "Why do I listen to her?"

He took out a wall grenade. The weapon was crafted for ruthless efficiency in tight corridors. Upon detonation, it released a shimmering wall of radiant energy that advanced down a corridor, disintegrating everything in its path. There was no way to hide from the wall of energy, which expanded to the edges of the passageway as it moved forward.

Lucius frowned. "Not very sporting of you is it? The captain know you have that?"

"Dead men don't bite."

Christian tossed the grenade into the hallway. A wall of energy ignited and moved off down the passageway, annihilating everything in its wake and scorching the walls. Screams echoed down the passageway. A moment later, all was quiet.

*   *   *

Seraphine and Jorge arrived at a long corridor with an arched opening on either end. She nodded at a panel on the wall. "Security corridor."

She activated a scanner built into her space suit. An intricate weave of light beams were revealed crisscrossing the passage. She withdrew a knife from its sheath and tossed it into the corridor. Hidden lasers fired, turning it into a chunk of melted metal.

Jorge smiled. "I hope you won't need that later."

Seraphine shrugged. "We'll have to use our shields."

"They won't last, Senora," he said. "We'll be trapped on the other side."

Seraphine felt her muscles tightening and furrowed her brow. "Stay here if you like."

Turning on her personal force field, Seraphine ran through the corridor. A dozen laser beams fired and struck the shield, but she passed through the corridor unharmed. Seraphine looked at the power indicator for her force field generator and noticed that it was low. Jorge cursed and ran through the corridor. Laser beams fired at him but were absorbed by his force field in a blinding flash of light.

* * *

The boarding party exchanged fire with the warbots guarding the command deck. Lucius took out a grenade and tossed it into the hallway. The detonation destroyed the warbots.

A moment later, soldiers from the *Ha Ni He* arrived from another passageway and took up defensive positions next to the destroyed warbots. Christian peered around the corner, took a shot and ducked back. He noticed that Lucius had stopped firing. "What is it?"

"My shield is out of power," said Lucius. "You think the captain would mind if I used something more lethal?

Christian smiled. "I'm a dog if I'm going to continue to play stun games with imperial soldiers. Do it. When I'm captain, you'll be first mate."

Lucius holstered his laser pistol and unslung his particle beam rifle. He peered around the corner and shot a stream of energized atomic particles. All of the soldiers outside the command deck were killed and the wall collapsed into a smoking hole. Lucius paused to smile at his handiwork.

Christian smiled, too. "Thank 'ee, kindly, sir."

A laser pulse darted out from the smoky doorway and struck Lucius in the shoulder. Christian pulled him out of the line of fire, to safety. Lucius slid down the wall to the floor, grunting in pain.

"There's a lot of cover behind that hole in the wall. You'll never get them all."

Christian pressed a switch on both of their space suits and their helmets materialized. He signaled for the others in their assault group to do the same. Christian set his laser rifle to fire a beam and smiled at Lucius. He laid down on the floor and rolled out into the hallway. "Bite me!"

Taking aim, he fired a steady beam of deadly laser light.

The laser beam streaked through the hole in the wall and hit the far wall, turning it red. The beam quickly burned a hole in the hull of the starship. Rapid decompression occurred as the air was sucked out into space. A heavy fog filled the command deck as the air cooled and condensed. Everyone on the command deck died in seconds.

*   *   *

Seraphine walked up to the doorway of the vault and waved her companion forward. "Can you open it, Jorge?"

"I'm on it, captain."

Jorge activated a wrist device and a holographic panel materialized before him. The device emitted a soft hum, efficiently scanning the vault's structure, and displaying a detailed, three-dimensional model of the locking mechanism. He observed the shifting projections with the detached precision of a technician, rotating the handle

15

methodically. As the image adjusted, he ensured the alignment was exact. After a brief moment of calculated observation, the vault door opened with a quiet, decisive click.

Ten thousand sunstones filled the vault, enough to power a legion of starships. Seraphine

Stepped cautiously into the room and activated several small drones. The drones flew over the long line of crystals, deploying hyper-dimensional energy nets. One by one, the sunstones were absorbed into the nets, vanishing into a pocket dimension. The drones converged in the center of the room, combining their collected cargo into a single bundle. With precision, one of the drones dropped a small bag into Seraphine's hand and she smiled. "Brilliant!"

Seraphine tossed the bag to Jorge, freeing her hands to recall the remaining drones.

He caught it effortlessly, his grin spreading wider, too wide—like a Cheshire cat on the brink of madness

A sudden, wicked realization struck her as the truth sank in. *Well, well, well. It looks like I'm not the only one who likes to play with puppets.* The thought twisted into a smile. Her eyes narrowed. Her gaze was like the flicker of a flame before it consumed everything in its path.

"Adios, hija," he purred, his voice dripping with malice.

Jorge slammed the vault door shut, sealing her inside. Seraphine rushed to it, pounding furiously with her fists. "Jorge! I'll send you head-long to everlasting hell if I ever —"

Christian's voice interrupted her fury. "Captain —"

She cut him off. "By fire and flame. Not now, Christian."

Seraphine activated her personal shield, methodically increasing the power until it glowed a deep, incandescent red. With a measured stride, she approached the vault door. As she made contact, the shield intensified, becoming a concentrated sphere of heat. The metal of the vault door resisted briefly, then began to melt away as the shield burned through it with methodical efficiency. She moved forward with deliberate slowness, the shield's heat cutting a precise path out of the vault.

*   *   *

Sentinel 12 fired the electromagnetic coil gun down the passageway at approaching targets. Gisele took cover and looked through the force field covered openings in the hull, out into space at their corsair, the *Lethe*. Most of the boarding party had retreated through space back to their starship. A slug of energized atomic particles struck Sentinel 12 and the warbot exploded. Gisele stared at the exit as her voice shook. "Christian, you son of a bastard, where are you?"

*   *   *

Seraphine advanced down the corridor. She came across Jorge's

17

body. It lay in the security corridor, cut to pieces by the hidden lasers. The hyper-dimensional bag containing the sunstones was on the floor, just beyond the security corridor. Glancing at the energy indicators in her space suit, she saw that her shield was nearly out of power. Exasperated, she activated her communicator. "What did you want to tell me, Christian?"

"We've taken the command deck but the crew got off a distress signal," he said. "An imperial man 'o war is on the way."

"You'd better get off the starship."

"Most of our crew are already away." Christian's voice had an edge of humor. "Would you like me to turn off the security field for you?"

A console by the entrance to the security corridor chimed. A red light turned green. The lasers powered down. Seraphine walked through the security corridor and picked up the bag of sunstones. She glanced at Jorge's burnt body. "Wanker."

* * *

Seraphine reached their designated exit point and surveyed the smoking ruins of the warbot Sentinel 12. Her eyes scanned the surroundings, but Gisele was nowhere to be seen. She turned, noticing through an energy wall that the *Lethe* had already sailed away.

Without warning, a security robot fired a laser, striking

Seraphine's shield. Instinctively, she ducked into a side passage. Drawing her laser pistol, she switched the setting to pulsed fire. A roll across the passage's opening took her to the opposite side. She aimed and fired. The pulse of laser energy hit the robot squarely, disabling it.

A second robot appeared from a nearby corridor, firing at her. The energy pulse penetrated her shield and shattered her pistol. Cursing under her breath, Seraphine grabbed her Vajra Thunderbolt baton from her belt. She closed her eyes, concentrating. Moments later, it transformed into a molecular-edged sword. Charging, she rapidly closed the distance to the robot and with one swift strike, cut it in two.

Breathing heavily, Seraphine leaned against the wall and closed her eyes, wondering what to do next. Footsteps echoed down the passageway. Her eyes snapped open just as Christian appeared, helping the injured Lucius along. She stepped forward to meet them. Christian looked outside through the energy barriers and noticed that the *Lethe* had gone. "Daughter of an envenomed witch, she is."

Her lips cured into a smile. "Yes, she is."

Seraphine spotted an approaching imperial man 'o war through the energy barriers. A communication crackled to life: "This is Captain David Corsini of the Vesuvio. Surrender yourselves."

Seraphine's eyes narrowed on the starship. *Come to play with me, have you?* A defiant grin spread across her face. "Devil take ye." With a dramatic flourish, she activated her space helmet and magnetic boots. Christian and Lucius did so, too.

Seraphine closed her eyes once more, focusing. Her Vajra Thunderbolt transformed again, this time into a mace with a flanged head. The weight of it felt unnatural, heavy. She stepped into the passageway, each movement fluid and carefree, as though she was twirling on air. Every step was a mockery, every sway a taunt.

She strode forward, dancing, and with a flourish, swung the mace at the force field blocking one of the breaches in the starship's hull. The barrier shattered with a violent burst of energy, dissipating into nothingness, as if it were a mere toy to be broken. A whirlwind of air surged into space, but Seraphine didn't flinch. Her grin widened, wild and free, a dancer on the edge of destruction. The others held fast, but Seraphine laughed, reveling in the storm she had just unleashed.

When the whirlwind had died down, Seraphine tossed the hyper-dimensional bag containing the sunstones into the void. It vanished into the blackness. She turned her gaze back to the *Vesuvio*, her smile fading away. "Your starships shall never drink from their dark crystalline wine."

*   *   *

CHAPTER TWO

The Monster

AZURE DRAGON OF THE EAST

HD 172051 / BIJON BLEU

A blanket of pain smothered her back, its weight oppressive, yet somehow dulled by its very multitude. It came from so many places, so many sources, that it had become a single, endless ache that threatened to swallow her whole. A cold breeze swept over her skin, its touch sharp as iron, a cruel contrast to the heat that burned through her body. She let out an involuntary whimper, though she despised herself for doing so.

Seraphine was parched, her throat a dry, cracked desert, and in the quiet of her mind, she dreamed of a river, cool and shimmering, its waters whispering promises of relief. It was a river of moonlight and stars, flowing just beyond her reach.

Something was holding up her arms, the sensation cold and unyielding.

Slowly, her eyes fluttered open, and the world around her came into focus—dark and unfamiliar. Her arms were held aloft, bound by metal rings that dug cruelly into her wrists. She was hanging from chains that stretched up to the ceiling, holding her suspended in the dim, silent space. Her blouse, once white, was torn open at the back, soaked with her own blood. It clung to her like a second skin, a reminder of her suffering. The pain flared again, sharper than before.

She didn't whimper this time.

A horrible scream swept down the hallway from another cell. It echoed in her mind, blocking out her own pain. Seraphine closed her eyes, not wanting to know who it was. All at once, lightning struck again and intense pain rippled through her back, causing an involuntary scream to escape from her lips. She glanced up at a cruel-faced man with a bloody whip in one hand. After the wave of pain had faded slightly, she forced herself to laugh out loud.

Laughter was her only weapon against them now.

Before the man with the whip could respond, she heard the creak of the cell door as it was opened. Another man walked in slowly, his hands stained with blood. He glanced down at her with a blank face. "The injured one has died," he said. "How long will it take for this one to die, I wonder?"

Lucius was dead. *Tortured to death.* Fury burned in her heart. It exploded into a scream. Seraphine lunged at the man, but the chains held her back. With a cloth, the man wiped the blood off his hands and yawned. She focused her eyes, peering through the darkness and recognized the man as Captain David Corsini. *So I am on his starship, the Vesuvio.*

Corsini reclined against a table, as relaxed as if he were on holiday. He nodded and her tormentor struck her with the whip again. Seraphine bit her lip, refusing to scream this time. The pain swept over her back and through her body like the tide washing over a beach.

Corsini smiled. "I see you have already met Giuseppe."

Gasping for breath, she nodded. "Yes."

Corsini picked up a pitcher from the table and poured water into a glass. He drank it down, letting out a loud sigh as he set the glass back down.

So this is the game we're playing, is it? He's just a clown without makeup. A smile crept into Seraphine's face. She couldn't help herself—she started laughing again.

Corsini's jaw tightened. "You are accused of piracy in a time of war."

Seraphine stopped laughing just to respond. "When is the Imperium not at war?"

Giuseppe struck her with the whip again. Seraphine whimpered at the pain. Blackness tugged at her, threatening to pull her into the darkness of unconsciousness. She took a few deep breaths. It helped a little.

"She's a stubborn one, captain," said Giuseppe.

"You and your comrades are to be executed," Corsini said. "What have you to say?"

Seraphine tilted her head, a slow smile spreading across her face. Her voice was measured, each word spoken with deliberate weight. "Civus Imperium Sum."

The words struck Corsini like a bolt of lightning, blinding and unforgiving. For a moment, he was paralyzed, unable to respond. The cell stood still, heavy with the silence that followed.

Seraphine laughed.

Incredulous, Corsini gaped at her with a dazed look. "You're a Pure Strain Human?"

Seraphine laughed some more.

Giuseppe shook his head.

Corsini's voice quivered. "No, no, no, this isn't happening!"

Giuseppe frowned. "What's wrong captain?"

Corsini's voice dropped to a whisper. "Didn't you hear? She's a citizen of the Imperium. As such she has the right to be tried on earth."

"Why not simply kill her?"

"We'll never get away with it. The Imperium tracks all Pure Strains," Corsini said. He shoved Giuseppe back and shouted, "Call for a healer, now!"

Seraphine laughed at her tormentors. "Perhaps they won't execute you."

Fury flashed across Giuseppe's face as he stepped toward Seraphine.

In that moment, Corsini's shout rang out, "No!"

Giuseppe struck her in the face and she fell into darkness.

* * *

3230 A.D. — YEAR OF THE METAL DOG
(FOUR YEARS AGO)
YELLOW DRAGON OF THE EARTH
THE FORBIDDEN PALACE — SOL / TERRA

Seraphine's bare feet whispered against the cold stone floor, each step a soft caress of the ancient surface. She followed Tribune William Parker down an ornate hallway with crimson walls. Carved dragons spiraled up the columns, their bodies twisting in intricate patterns that flickered faintly in the dim light. The air smelled faintly of incense, the sweet, earthy aroma weaving through the high arches above them. Candles danced from inside hanging lanterns, throwing long shadows against the walls. The temple fortress had been constructed thousands of years ago, but still held an air of mysticism, as if the souls of the ancient priests still resided there. They both wore the white uniform of a centurion, though they went barefoot.

They passed through an alcove where a small, polished fountain murmured, its water flowing over smooth stones into a shallow basin. The sound seemed to slow their steps, drawing them deeper into the temple's calm. To the left, a door stood slightly ajar, revealing a small meditation room, the floor strewn with mats and cushions. The hallway widened into a second chamber, a vast room with high ceilings supported by thick wooden beams.

William spoke, "A thousand years ago, there were many distinct styles of martial arts. The ancient systems were composed of lists of movements, memorized through practice. Each movement was performed separately, halting after each motion."

Seraphine frowned at the notion of memorizing movement patterns. How could one step into the flow of the universe with such a limited approach? "That's hard to believe."

They continued on, the path narrowing again, leading them into a hall where the floor was worn smooth, the stones pitted and aged from generations of practice. The walls here were adorned with faded tapestries depicting scenes of martial mastery, centurions in graceful poses locked in combat with unseen adversaries.

William continued, "If you remove the stops, you will have continuous movement, spontaneous instead of memorized, fluid and no longer rigid. This connects us to True Source in a way which was not possible before."

Seraphine thought of ancient martial arts systems, where the movements were like the jagged edges of a broken river, each step a separate rock that halted the flow of water. They memorized patterns of motion, separated by stops—stills in time that disrupted the natural rhythm of the body. The Tao Phi was superior, of course, like a river that flowed endlessly, its current unbroken, seamless, weaving around obstacles without pause. Continuous, fluid, adapting with every twist and turn.

They exited the building and walked outside into a vast court-yard where the sun, golden and soft as an old quilt, spilled across the cobblestones, warming the air with the smell of the earth. Recruits danced through the light, training with their Vajra Thunderbolt batons—small gleaming rods that shimmered and sparkled, trans-forming into different kinds of weapons.

William continued, "In the ancient world the priority was self-defense, but it devolved into systems of destruction. It descend-ed to a place of ego and competition, becoming more violent and destructive."

Seraphine threw a glance at her instructor. "Isn't all warfare destructive?"

"Perhaps," he said. "The centurions are not just a military force, Seraphine. After the fall of the Republic, we reformed martial arts into the Tao Phi, a source of creative energy. By mimicking nature, we became a conduit for love."

They walked by a centurion practicing with a thunderbolt spear. He conducted a series of acrobatic maneuvers, followed by a flurry of attacks. William said, "There are three kinds of centurions: Guardians, Light Bringers and Messengers of Love."

They passed a centurion training with a thunderbolt axe. He transformed the axe into a mace and struck a stone column in the center of the courtyard. The impact cracked the stone, sending a sharp echo through the air, but the training column held firm. The centurion twirled around and transformed his thunderbolt into a sword. William pointed at him. "Guardians protect humanity," he said. "They are the least powerful of the centurions."

They walked by a centurion who transformed his Vajra Thunderbolt into a bladed staff. William and Seraphine paused a moment to watch. After a series of twirling movements, he came to rest. An owl, its wings silent, glided down to perch atop the temple roof. Its yellow eyes regarded them, as if pondering their words. "Light

Bringers devote their lives to truth," said William. "They are the wisest."

They continued on their way and passed by a centurion twirling a thunderbolt baton. A thousand flower petals appeared out of nowhere, drifting to the ground. A surge of warmth filled Seraphine, a quiet joy that made the world seem lighter. William watched the petals fall and smiled. "Messengers of Love, the most powerful, spread healing and love."

Seraphine raised her eyebrows in curiosity. "Which kind of centurion are you, sir, and what kind will I become?"

"I dance the path of a Light Bringer," he said. "You must choose your own dance with enlightenment. This is how you will discover your destiny."

A passing cloud threw the courtyard into shadows. A gentle breeze came, disturbing the wind chimes hanging from the roof of the nearest building. Seraphine paused to listen to them. Inharmonic sounds banished evil spirits.

William pointed at a thunderbolt. "The Vajra Thunderbolt is the instrument of a centurion. It symbolizes both the properties of a diamond and a bolt of thunder."

Seraphine nodded. "Indestructibility and irresistible force."

"Yes," he said. "In the hands of a centurion trained in its use, a Vajra Thunderbolt transforms an ordinary person into the most powerful force in the universe. A centurion does not fight solely against flesh and blood, but against the spirits of darkness. The ancient races spoke of dark beings who had the power to possess individuals. The Archons, and their enemies, the Eloiein."

"Who were the Archons?" she asked.

"They were an ancient race. After conquering the galaxy, they found enlightenment and ascended into heaven. Lord Anshar and Queen Eiris were the last rulers of the Archons."

Seraphine nodded. "So they are all extinct."

William shrugged and turned to look at the clouds in the sky. "I think some of the ancients are out there still. Centurions sometimes encounter people who are possessed by evil spirits." He smiled at the fascination in her eyes. "The Vajra Thunderbolt is a sacred weapon in spiritual warfare."

The clouds drifted away and the sun came out again.

William and Seraphine stopped, their eyes drawn to the centurions as they moved. Each centurion's style reflected the essence of their soul. One's movements were like a rushing river, swift and unyielding; another, fluid and precise, as if carved from stone; yet another moved with the grace of wind, each strike a whisper. The clash of their Vajra Thunderbolts were a symphony of strength, wisdom and inner peace.

Seraphine glanced at the thunderbolt hanging from William's

belt. "How is a thunderbolt used, sifu?"

William said, "A centurion learns to sense living vortices of energy by aligning their chi, their life force, to True Source through movements that emanate from nature's golden spiral, the Fibonacci Sequence. It focuses a toroidal energy field, a vortex of life energy inside it. The physics will fold around it because it is a continuum of energy. Like a river which is powerful because of the water flowing through it, a thunderbolt will give you power."

The courtyard dance was calming, as if they were watching a performance.

"By seeking the path of least resistance. Conflict is a non issue. We merely arrive," said William. "Through movement, we become a vessel of servitude for the greater good of the universe. This is the essence of self mastery."

William picked up his thunderbolt baton and executed a series of flowing movements while the thunderbolt transformed into different kinds of weapons. "This is the Tao Phi. This is the way of chi. This is the way of energy, life force, as well as gravity, water, magnetics, electricity, and love. All these are properties of energy potentials as we are expanding and contracting within the human form."

Finally, he ended the display and retracted the thunderbolt into a baton. "This baton is the thunderbolt of enlightenment. It is the key to the unseen realms of True Source. There is an infinity right here."

William handed the thunderbolt baton to Seraphine. She frowned. "My thunderbolt has never performed these miracles, sir. It is simply a staff or a sword in my hands."

"The thunderbolt is connected to your consciousness," he said. "It will give you more powers as you discover greater spiritual truths."

Seraphine looked out over the courtyard, past the walls of the fortress, into the mountains. "Why does it grant more lethal weapons to those who are more enlightened?"

William's voice drew her attention back to him. "Power should only be given to those who understand its consequences."

* * *

3234 A.D. — YEAR OF THE WOOD TIGER (PRESENT DAY)
AZURE DRAGON OF THE EAST
HD 172051 / BIJON BLEU

Seraphine awakened to a new cell which was in a row along a passageway. The outer walls were transparent, revealing a field of stars outside. The planet Bijon Bleu was below. Steel bars, reinforced by force fields covered the exits. Christian was in an adjacent cell, and another man sat in a cell opposite. He controlled a kind of dark charisma and had the look of a predator. But he had a vacant look in his eyes.

Seraphine sat up and realized that all of her injuries were gone. She noticed that her captors had dressed her in a new blouse, too. It was the same kind of blouse which had worn as part of an imperial uniform. She had an urge to take it off. "Where are we?"

Resigned to his fate, Christian had a complacent look in his eyes. "They transferred us to the Persephone. A man 'o war with seventy-four guns. They must think we're important."

Seraphine looked into his blue eyes. For a moment, she wondered why he, too, had been brought here and not summarily executed. "Citizens of the Imperium are important," she grumbled. "Where's Galen?"

"A dozen good fellows of our crew are dead," he said. "Galen too."

Seraphine stood up, angry. She paced back and forth in her cell. "How could you let simple provincial citizens kill them? What happened?"

Christian calmly replied, "You told me to go easy on them, so we walked right into a trap. They had a disintegrator. Galen and many more are dead because of you."

Seraphine sat down again. "I can't accept that."

"That's what happens when you attack well armed military supply ships."

33

"So, they resisted you?"

His smile was full of fire. "I took care of 'em. It was fun."

Seraphine hugged her legs. "Sometimes you frighten me, Christian."

He laughed. "Shocked at the brutality of mankind, are you?"

She shook her head. "I have never killed anyone in cold blood."

"You've never killed anyone?" he asked. "A pirate captain like you?"

Seraphine laughed. "Does genocide count?"

"Be serious."

"I am serious when I asked you not to kill. All human life is precious."

Christian smirked. "Don't you mean to say that all life is precious?"

She gave out a quick, disgusted snort. "Don't be silly," she said. "The fate of alien inferiors is inconsequential."

Christian glared at her. "There weren't any inferiors on that transport. Just humans."

Seraphine looked through the transparent walls at the empty stars. Bijon Blu had fallen into night and the cities there lit up the darkness. The blue-skinned aquatic aliens that lived on the water world called themselves the Sakle. They had submitted to the Imperium immediately when humans had landed there. *Peace is always better than warfare.* Her voice dropped to a whisper. "Did you have to kill them all?"

"Have you considered what will happen out on the frontier when they don't get sunstones to power their fleets of starships? Hundreds of thousands of people will die."

An imperial legion was composed of ten thousand starships and had a million men and women serving, along with three to five times as many warbots. The legions protected hundreds of millions of people living on the imperial colonies. Seraphine clenched her teeth. "People will die only if the Imperium continues with their wars."

He chuckled. "So this is political. I thought you were just greedy, like me."

She shook her head. "Doesn't matter anymore. Our pirating days are over."

He crossed his arms. "Not me. I'm going to continue my life of crime," he said. "We should go back to hitting regular merchant ships with robot crews."

Seraphine had taken his earlier resignation as a sign that he had given up. She was wrong. He was as determined as ever to escape.

"Did Jorge make it?" he asked.

"No."

He shook his head. "He was a good man, to be sure."

She had an urge to hit something. "He left me to die."

Christian looked away from her, out through the transparent walls of their prison, into space and sighed. "I suppose you can't trust anyone these days."

"Seraphine's eyes shifted over to the stranger. He had long dark hair that fell over his shoulders in a wild entanglement, dark eyes and the shadow of a beard. "Who is this?"

Christian looked at the other captive. "His name is Sebastian Drake."

Seraphine raised her eyebrows. "Is that all?"

Sebastian's husky voice was was smooth as silk. "They took away all of my memories."

The door to the cell block opened and an attractive man entered, wearing the uniform of an imperial tribune. He had short black hair and intelligent eyes. His tunic was embroidered with the image of an avenging angel. He carried Seraphine's thunderbolt baton. A similar weapon hung from his own belt. As he strolled over, Seraphine looked at him with a mixture of desire and resentment. He was accompanied by a coy, young woman, in a uniform. She had a brightness about her that reminded Seraphine of a star shining in the darkness. The light followed her like a shadow. The woman also carried a thunderbolt baton, the weapon of a centurion.

The man stopped in front of Seraphine's cell and he smiled

down at her.

"Him the Almighty Power

Hurld headlong flaming from th' Ethereal Skie

With hideous ruine and combustion down

To bottomless perdition, there to dwell

In adamantine chains and penal fire."

Seraphine looked away from him and into the field of stars outside. "Quoting Milton again, Lieutenant?"

"I am a tribune, now, Seraphine." He examined her Vajra Thunderbolt. "When Corsini reported he'd captured a pirate in possession of a thunderbolt, I thought to myself, 'What's a pirate doing with a centurion's thunderbolt?' But when he reported that he'd captured a citizen of the Imperium I knew it was you."

"What do you want, Dominic?"

"Where did you hide the sunstones?"

Seraphine laughed. "Aren't you going to introduce me to your companion?"

Dominic smiled. "Seraphine DeVere, this is Lieutenant Inanna Silva."

Inanna drew her thunderbolt, transformed it into a sword, saluted and performed an elegant curtsy. Dropping to one knee, she bowed her head for a moment and raised it up again. A grin lit up her face and she straightened up again.

Seraphine raised her eyebrows. "You're a centurion?"

Inanna nodded. "Yes." Transforming her thunderbolt back into a baton, Inanna hung it back onto her belt.

Seraphine and Inanna glared at one another. Inanna had the look of an innocent child but also had an air of mischievousness. It was as if she considered everything to be a joke. Seraphine wondered why she served as Dominic's Optio Centurion, his primary subordinate, and how she had attained such a position.

Dominic broke the silence. "What are you doing out here, Seraphine?"

A voice came from the other cell. "You'll get nothing out of us."

Christian's remark brought their attention. Dominic turned to look at him. "Provincial citizens should respect their betters, even pirates."

Dominic activated a control on his belt and all of the air in Christian's cell began to drain away into space. Inanna giggled, enjoying the spectacle. Dominic turned around to face Seraphine once more. "The ancients believed that God threw us out of paradise, that we're fallen beings with an evil nature."

Seraphine looked at Christian, wondering if Dominic was going to let him die.

Dominic continued, "Nonsense, I say. Such a world has never existed. Eden is a myth.

If we ever lived in darkness it was brought on by our own weaknesses."

Christian gasped for air. Inanna looked on, smiling, as if it was all a game.

Dominic looked into Seraphine's eyes. "Remember when you and I used to dream of finding a new Eden? A world untainted by inferior aliens. A pure world, where humanity could learn to love again."

Christian fell down and faded away into unconsciousness.

Dominic was too intent on Seraphine to notice or care about Christian. "You were once a bright, shining star. Your defiance is bewildering."

Seraphine shouted at him, "I threw the sunstones into space!"

Dominic stood up straight. After a moment's hesitation, he pressed the device on his belt. The air was pumped back into the cell. Christian sat up, gulping air. Inanna frowned in disappointment. "Ooh."

Dominic leaned against the wall of Seraphine's cell and lowered his voice, more intimate this time. "You could have been great you know."

Christian recovered and sat up. "Please, please, please, please, please leave!"

Dominic smiled, turned around and strode towards the exit,

followed by Inanna. His voice echoed off the transparent walls that looked out into the emptiness of space.

"A dungeon horrible, on all sides round

As one great furnace flam'd, yet from those flames

No light, but rather darkness visible

Serv'd only to discover sights of woe,

Regions of sorrow, doleful shades, where peace

And rest can never dwell."

The door at the end of the corridor slid shut with a bang.

* * *

CHAPTER THREE
The Enchantress

AZURE DRAGON OF THE EAST

HD 172051 / BIJON BLEU

Like a breath of fresh air, soft footsteps approached. Seraphine saw a beautiful girl, with pale skin and long blonde hair. She wore a blue bindi jewel on her forehead, a garland of orchids and a delicate white dress. A medallion of unusual metal hung from her neck and a translator earring hung from her ear. The girl was impossibly beautiful, a goddess among fashion models. Seraphine saw Christian in the other cell sit up, his eyes full of wonder.

The girl was a ghost, a whisper out of a nightmare, drifting in on the air like smoke from a forgotten fever. Seraphine began to tremble. Her stomach twisted painfully, and her heart tightened, each beat a heavy reminder she couldn't shake. She squeezed her eyes shut, hoping the image of the girl would disappear, but it lingered. A heavy weight gnawed at her, crawling beneath her skin, settling deep in the pit of her stomach.

Seraphine wanted to move, to escape, but there was nowhere to run. She could hear the soft, measured steps, the breathless whispers, the way the girl's presence lingered in the air like perfume. It was a reminder that she couldn't run far enough, couldn't outrun the weight of what hung in the air. Seraphine pressed her palm against her forehead, struggling to calm the rising panic, to ground herself. She couldn't look back, couldn't face the girl—not now. The contrast between the girl's innocent beauty and the raw, unsettled knot twisting inside her was unbearable. She turned away and kept her eyes shut.

* * *

3232 A.D. — YEAR OF THE WATER RAT (TWO YEARS AGO) AZURE DRAGON OF THE EAST — HD 154088 / IOUNN

A beautiful blue planet, Iounn, was a jewel in the darkness. Turquoise oceans and green forests covered the world. On the night side, town lights pierced the darkness. A starship, the *Brandywine*, orbited the planet.

Wearing the uniform of an Imperial Scout Captain, Seraphine

42

stepped out onto the star deck, one hand dripping blood. She walked over to the command chair as a robot slave approached with a silver tray holding a bowl of water and towel. She removed a ring from her finger and threw it onto the tray. She washed the blood from her hand, dried it and waved the slave away.

Seraphine sat down and a second robot slave approached with a silver tray holding a crystal glass and a bottle of champagne. The robot popped open the bottle and filled the glass. After a moment's hesitation, Seraphine picked it up. The slave retreated.

In the viewscreen a nuclear flash appeared on the surface of the planet. Slowly, more and more flashes appeared adjacent to the first flash. A nuclear firestorm began to gradually spread over the world, a creeping wall of fire and death, taking its time to devour the planet.

Seraphine sipped champagne slowly, like a connoisseur, lingering on the taste.

It was a celebration.

*　*　*

3234 A.D. — YEAR OF THE WOOD TIGER (PRESENT DAY)
AZURE DRAGON OF THE EAST
HD 172051 / BIJON BLEU

The girl's voice was a melody woven from summer rain, light and clear. It filled the air with something both sweet and untouchable. Each syllable fluttered like a bird's wing, leaving a trace of innocence in its wake. "You are the pirate, Seraphine DeVere?"

Opening her eyes, Seraphine saw the girl looking down at her with curiosity. The girl had walked up to the energy barrier that kept the prisoners inside, a faint ripple in the air marking the edge of her reach. Seraphine could see her own reflection faintly in the smooth surface of the energy barrier.

The girl's voice was soft, gentle. "Would you like to leave?"

The prison was silent, save for the faint hum of the energy fields covering the cells. Since the walls of the cell block were transparent, it felt as though they were sitting outside under a field of stars. As the starship slowly rotated on its axis toward the stars, the planet Bijon Bleu sank below the horizon. Endless stars scattered across the blackness like diamonds in the dark.

All Seraphine wanted to do was run away, which wasn't possible. Like a caged tiger, she erupted in rage, shouting at the girl, "Get away from me!"

The girl stepped back a pace. She tilted her head, not understanding Seraphine's reaction. "You do not wish to escape from this place?"

Seraphine's voice was cold. "You are an inferior. Leave us!"

Christian looked at Seraphine with surprise. "Inferior? Captain, she's not an alien!"

Seraphine stood up. "I know an alien when I see one."

44

Christian got up too. "Ignore her! I want to leave. Can you open my cell door?"

The girl activated a device encircling her wrist and all of the force fields in the prison corridor vanished. Christian and Sebastian stepped out of their cells. The girl handed a bag to Christian. "Here are some of your belongings."

Christian withdrew Seraphine's thunderbolt and a holster containing his laser pistol from the bag. He buckled the weapon on.

Seraphine remained in her cell, unmoving.

Christian walked up and snapped his fingers in Seraphine's face. "Hey stupid, come on!"

As if waking from a dream, Seraphine left her cell.

*   *   *

The landing bay of the *Persephone* held a variety of auxiliary craft—launches, pinnaces, cutters and skiffs. A longboat zipped through the energy barrier that kept out the vacuum of space and landed. A moment after, the crew disembarked and exited through a door on the far side of the landing bay. A guard stood watch by the nearest entrance.

Seraphine observed from the shadowed corner, her eyes narrowing as the girl led them towards the entrance, pausing just around the corner, out of the guard's sight. Sebastian crept forward like a panther, his movements fluid and measured. "I'll take care of him."

45

But the girl raised her hand, a delicate command in the stillness. "Wait."

Sebastian halted.

The girl approached the security guard with the grace of a fairy, her steps light, yet deliberate, as though she were walking through a dream of her own making. The guard, oblivious to everything but her presence, stood motionless, his eyes glassy, as if pulled into a trance. He seemed to forget the world around him.

She smiled. "Guess what happened?"

The guard blinked and furrowed his brow. "What?"

"I've been thinking a lot about what you said yesterday," she murmured, her words lingering in the air like threads woven into a dream.

The security guard was perplexed. "What did I say?"

The girl leaned in slightly, her voice dropping into a conspiratorial whisper. "You must remember," she said. "It's a subject of great importance that will shape the future of humanity."

His eyes drifted over her beauty. "Oh, yeah?"

The girl nodded slowly, a subtle, knowing glint in her eyes. "It's easy to remember but you need to focus. Let's do this. Step outside for a few minutes and it'll come back to your mind. Then return to me. I'll be here waiting. We'll discover the true meaning together."

The security guard nodded in agreement. "I'll see you soon."

With a soft shuffle of his boots, he turned and walked away down the passageway, out of sight. Seraphine remained frozen, her mind racing as the faint echo of his footsteps faded.

The girl waved at the pirates and they went over to the entrance of the landing bay.

Christian shook his head, as if to clear it. "How did she —"

Sebastian put his hand on Christian's shoulder. "Does it matter?"

"Yes."

Seraphine pointed to a small starship. "That cutter will do nicely," she said. "Lets away."

*   *   *

The ramp rose and sealed behind them with a precise hiss, the familiar vibration of the cutter's engines reverberating through the hull. Seraphine slid into her seat with practiced ease, her gaze fixed on the controls. Christian took the wheel of the helm while Sebastian and the girl sat down in passenger seats.

Seraphine activated the command console and the planet Bijon Bleu appeared in the viewscreen in a burst of soft light. With a casual wave of her hand, she brought up a holographic display of the surrounding star system. The *Persephone* rapidly shrank behind them.

The planet lay dreaming in the night. Its surface glimmered

softly, shrouded in a thin veil of clouds and mist. Oceans stretched across its face, reflecting the cold beauty of the stars. Christian pointed at Bijon Bleu. "We can land there without being noticed. I know a way to —"

Seraphine interrupted, "No, head for the third moon of the ninth planet."

Christian's response was automatic. "Aye, aye, captain."

Reluctantly, he extended the solar sails of the cutter. Three masts extended from the cylindrical hull. The solar sails unfurled. They glittered like silver flower petals as they caught the light of the star HD 172051. He leaned back in his chair. "They'll track us. If we drop into the atmosphere of the planet they'll never find us."

The girl's voice was like the soft murmur of a brook, gentle and pure, as if the wind itself had learned to speak. "Don't worry about them."

Christian swiveled around in his seat to stare at the girl.

Seraphine continued to examine the viewscreen, unwilling to look at her directly.

The girl carried herself with the grace of an aristocrat, her posture poised as she spoke with calm assurance. "I have disabled their weapons."

Christian smiled . "What's your name, friend?"

The girl closed her eyes and whispered, "I am Inglina

Nivienne."

"Why are you helping us?" asked Christian.

"I wanted to leave," said Ingli.

Seraphine shot a glance at Christian. "Proceed Mr. Thiessen. Take us to the ninth planet."

The cutter sailed away from the *Persephone*, away into space.

*   *   *

Dominic walked into the center of a ring with three men holding Vajra Thunderbolt swords while Inanna looked on. He fastened a blindfold over his eyes and took up a fighting stance. One by one, the three men attacked. Dodging the first strike, he stepped aside and struck under the neck of his first attacker. The man fell flat onto his back. Dominic spun around, ducked a sword slash and knocked out his second attacker. The third man ran forward and swung down with his sword. Dominic stepped close, blocked the man's hand and struck him with a paralyzing blow. He threw the man over his shoulders and onto the floor.

Dominic removed his blindfold with satisfaction. After the integration of his cybernetic enhancements, he had transcended the limits of human capability. His body moved with the precision of a well-oiled machine, faster than thought, stronger than steel, and with a mind honed by neural processors that calculated his every move with clinical accuracy. Since he had chosen to undergo the process of becoming an enhanced human, no foe had even come close to challenging his dominance. Defeat had become an abstract concept, something relegated to the distant past, overshadowed by the certainty of his superiority.

Inanna stepped into the ring with a smirk on her face.

He grinned back.

She drew her thunderbolt and transformed it into a staff.

He drew his Vajra Thunderbolt and turned it into a staff as well.

She advanced upon him, throwing a series of blows, faster than anyone he had ever fought before.

He retreated, parried and had to tumble out of the way.

As he got up, she struck out, quick as a panther, tripping him.

Dominic ended up on the deck.

For the first time, defeat washed over him like a cold, unrelenting tide. The shock of the loss reverberated in his mind, a dissonant note that echoed through every fiber of his being. He lay there motionless for a moment, the world around him distant, as if he were observing someone else's failure, not his own. The weight of it settled in, deep and insistent, but there was no time for reflection. Only the gnawing realization that everything he had known about himself had suddenly unraveled. The invincibility he had worn like a mantle was no more.

Inanna straddled him. Transforming her Vajra Thunderbolt

into a curved knife, she held it up to his throat.

For a brief instant, a touch of fear threatened to turn into a panic.

Inanna grinned, enjoying the power she held over him.

She was lucky, that's all. He shook off the fear and grinned back.

Inanna said, "You've always told me to treat your superior as a master, your equal as a rival and your inferior as a servant."

"That is a centurion's motto," he said. "Do you have a problem with it?"

She laughed. "Am I inferior to you?"

Dominic flipped her over onto her back and he let his body press against hers.

She let out a seductive whimper and let go of the thunderbolt. It fell to the deck, shifting from a knife back into a small baton.

He smiled down at her, intoxicated by her beauty.

She leaned her head up to kiss him.

Before their lips could touch, the intercom chimed. He pushed her down, got up and activated his communicator. "What is it?"

The voice of Captain Flavius Septimus was full of concern. "Sir, the pirates are missing, along with the alien who was in our care. They stole a cutter and escaped."

Dominic's voice was calm. "Destroy it."

"Sir, all of our weapons are offline."

51

A sigh escaped Dominic's lips. "All right. Go after them. Full pursuit."

"Aye, aye, sir."

Inanna rose to her feet. For a brief moment, Dominic's gaze caught a strange, ethereal presence beside her, like a shadow, but not of darkness. It had an almost imperceptible silhouette, its edges soft and shimmering like sunlight on water. It leaned towards her, a silent whisper in the stillness. Inanna nodded, her gaze steady, as if acknowledging a secret. Dominic blinked as the radiant figure faded into nothingness, leaving only the quiet hum of the room. The glittering phantom was gone.

He went over to a table, splashed water onto his face, then dried off with a towel, draping it around his neck as he took a slow, steadying breath.

Inanna looked down at her Vajra Thunderbolt for a moment before hanging it from her belt. "Tribune, I think there are better ways to use a thunderbolt."

Tossing the towel away, Dominic chuckled. "Indeed?"

Inanna nodded, all serious now. "Yes," she said. "You once told me that the Vajra Thunderbolt is a conduit for True Source. Wouldn't it be better to ignore God's guidance?"

They went out of the gymnasium and walked down a corridor. "That would invalidate it's purpose," he said.

"You will never master it," she insisted. "It's there to test you. In fact, it controls you."

Dominic shrugged. "The thunderbolt will always remain a mystery."

As they came to a door, Inanna stopped and put her hand on his shoulder. "I say ignore what it tells you," she said. "Follow your own path. Make it bend to your will."

Dominic gently removed her hand from his shoulder. "I would have to abandon my faith," he said. "What you suggest is an impure thing."

A delightful expression filled her face. "Just imagine for a moment, falling into darkness," she whispered. "Falling, down, down, into uncertainty. Spread your arms out and you could fly. Total, absolute, freedom. No restrictions, no one controlling you."

"Temptation is a dangerous thing," he said. "Come on."

The door opened and they stepped out onto the star deck.

*   *   *

As the cutter skimmed the surface of the moon orbiting the ninth planet, the silhouette of the *Lethe* emerged, nestled within the vast expanse of a deep crater. The cutter's solar sails folded inward, their gleaming surfaces dimming against the blackness of space. The cutter shifted its course, descending steadily toward the crater's floor. It touched down within the hangar of the corsair.

Seraphine walked down the gangplank from the cutter and stepped out onto the hangar bay of her starship. Gisele was there, waiting. Seraphine raised her eyebrows. "Did you get them?"

"Aye, captain. All of the sunstones are in our hold."

Seraphine wanted to make sure that the bag had been emptied. If a hyper-dimensional bag was actively holding contents while a starship entered hyperspace, it would cause a dimensional rift, destroying the starship. Most hyper-dimensional containers had a safety, and would automatically eject their contents just before a starship entered hyperspace, but if the hold wasn't big enough, some items would be lost forever, trapped inside the other dimension. "Good work, Sela."

Gisele looked at the cutter. "How many of you got away?"

Seraphine didn't want to tell her about how many of their crew had died. She shook her head. Christian, Sebastian and Ingli exited the cutter and Seraphine put a hand on Gisele's shoulder. "We have a few passengers," she said. Then lowered her voice so only Gisele could hear it. "The girl is extremely dangerous. Place a robot sentry over her immediately."

Gisele stared at Ingli. "She looks harmless to me."

"She is an enchantress" Seraphine's voice turned hot. "Do as I say."

"Aye, aye, captain."

Christian paused in front of Gisele with his hands upon his hips. "Have you tuned the hypersails? We should get under way as soon as possible."

Outside, through the energy barrier protecting the hold, Seraphine saw their pursuer approaching. Seraphine shouted, "Come on!"

* * *

The *Persephone* approached the moon. The *Lethe* fired thrusters to gain speed quickly and deployed solar sails. The *Persephone* fired a broadside of laser cannons. Pulses of laser light struck the surface of the moon, throwing up silent puffs of debris into the thin atmosphere. Before they could fire another broadside, the corsair slipped over the horizon of the moon and out of danger.

* * *

The *Lethe* glided through the darkness, a phantom among the stars. Its hull, painted an obsidian black, seemed to drink in the stars, absorbing their light until none was reflected back. Crafted from a composite of adaptive materials, the starship's surface shifted imperceptibly, refracting light in subtle ways that made it hard to distinguish from the surrounding emptiness. It wasn't invisible. It was there, but it was never truly seen. To mask it's heat trail, the engines, housed within a network of advanced thermal dampeners, released their energy in silent bursts, their presence barely a whisper against the cold vacuum. The starship's power output was masked by electromagnetic dampeners, erasing all traces of its electrical activity as though it was a ghost among shadows. Around it, the fabric of space twisted just slightly. A faint ripple in the gravitational field distorted sensors that relied on shifts in mass, making the starship seem not quite solid.

A transparent force field covered the star deck of the *Lethe*. Three sets of three masts radiated from the central hull, giving the corsair the appearance of a flower in bloom. The masts rose up through the transparent hull and into space, where the solar sails caught the light of the star. Star riggers climbed into tubes and up into the web of sails.

Seraphine stood on the quarterdeck, peering through a digitally enhanced spyglass at the horizon of the moon. *Try to catch me, Dominic*, she thought, a dark smile creeping across her face. It was like playing hide and seek as a ghost—one he would never find.

A holographic image displayed the starship's cathedral, which housed the hypersails under an acoustic dome inside an atmospheric chamber. Gisele was there, bathed in red light. With closed eyes, she tuned into the celestial spirit of the star and sang a beautiful melody, which modulated the harmonic frequencies in the air. The crystals lining the surfaces of the hyper sails responded to the music and shifted, aligning to catch light from the star. Seraphine listened to

Gisele's beautiful music while scanning for their pursuer.

A few paces away, a robot with a built-in laser stood guard over Ingli, who studiously ignored it. Sebastian Drake stood silently next to the captain. Down below, on the star deck, Christian paced back and forth, giving orders. "Look alive, man! Cut out the sheets."

The crew diminished the amount of sails exposed to the solar wind. On the quarterdeck behind Seraphine, stood the helm officer, Pranay Doshi. Seraphine gave him an order, "Down helm."

Pranay repeated the command. "Down helm. Aye aye, Ma'am." He turned the wheel, directing the starship to turn into the solar wind, slowing it down. The *Lethe* slipped into the shadow of a crater on the moon once again. Through the spyglass, Seraphine saw the *Persephone* as it glided by overhead. She lowered the spyglass just as the imperial warship fired blind, down at the moon. Stray shots bombarded the surface, throwing dust up into space.

Christian's voice came over the intercom. "Stealth mode is operational. It's working, captain."

Of course it worked. The Lethe was one of the most advanced stealth ships in the Imperium. Seraphine shut the spyglass. *Oh, darling, did you think I'd really stick around for your party?* She chuckled softly to herself. "You can't fight what you can't catch."

The *Persephone* flew away into space. Laser beams probed the darkness, firing blindly, hoping to strike their hidden target.

Sailing Master Nilay Thakur walked onto the quarterdeck. "Captain DeVere, are you come? I'm glad to see ye. I've been looking out for ye for a great while."

Seraphine knew that he wanted Christian's job as quartermaster, and wondered if their rivalry would ever come to blows. "I'm all seized over with joy at seeing your friendly face again, Mr. Thakur. Give me a view of the astrospheric current sheet for this star system."

The astrosphere, created by the million kilometer per hour stellar winds, was the vast bubble of magnetism that shielded star systems from deadly cosmic rays. "Aye, aye, captain."

He activated the holographic map which showed the ripples in the astrosphere created by the star's rotating magnetic field. It was a map of the supersonic stellar wind currents throughout the star system. The astrospheric current sheet was like an ancient coastline map, highlighting dangerous shallows and reefs. It was essential for travel within a star system.

Gisele, finished with tuning the hypersails, walked out onto the quarterdeck. "They repaired their weapons rather quickly."

Seraphine looked through the spyglass at the departing imperial man o' war and smiled. "Captain Dominic Fontaine is a tribune. He commands a hundred centurions. He's more capable than an average man."

Christian's voice came over the intercom. "We're ready, captain.

Say the word."

For a moment, she felt a wild, dangerous impulse—to stay, to toy with Dominic like a cat with a mouse. *A little more fear, a pinch of panic from the crew, and a dash of spicy frustration from Dominic— how deliciously tempting.* The thought of dragging it out, watching them all twist with anxiety, their minds scrambling, almost made her smile. But then, she realized, *I am the mouse.* The cat would catch her soon enough. Seraphine snapped the spyglass shut, a wicked grin tugging at the corners of her lips. *No, no. It's always best to leave a man hungry for more.* "Let's get out of here, Mr. Thiessen."

Christian shouted at the crew, "Crowd on sail and let her run before the wind!"

*   *   *

Several hours later, the *Lethe* approached the energy barrier at the edge of the star system. The *Persephone* wasn't far behind, and it fired it's bow guns at the fleeing starship.

On the quarterdeck, Seraphine watched as bolts of laser light flew past the starship. Sebastian looked nervous. "Why can't we simply enter the vortex?"

Nilay shook his head. "It's highly dangerous to transition into a hyperspace wormhole from within the astrosphere of a star."

Christian's voice came over the intercom, "Brace for termination shock."

The termination shock was the point in the astrosphere where the stellar wind slowed down to subsonic speeds, relative to the star, due to interactions with the local interstellar medium. This led to compression, heating, and a shift in the magnetic field. The termination shock was a standing shock wave.

The *Lethe* passed through the termination shock and entered the astrosheath, where the solar wind slowed down, compressed, and became turbulent due to its interaction with the interstellar medium. The *Lethe* shook in the tumult.

Nilay said, "We've entered the hydrogen wall."

Laser beams from the *Persephone* reached out, barely missing the *Lethe*. Seraphine chuckled. *No, Dominic. We'll waltz together another time.*

The starship was tossed about and then settled down as it passed through the wall of energized hydrogen into deep space. They had reached the astropause, the boundary where the stellar wind was halted by the interstellar medium.

Christian's voice came over the intercom. "We're beyond the hydrogen wall. Plasma density and the galactic cosmic rays have increased," he said. "We're pristine, captain."

Seraphine smiled. "Retract the solar sails and extend the hyper sails."

"Aye, aye, captain," said Nilay.

The solar sails retracted into the cathedral and the larger hyper sails extended out into space. The starship changed from a fairy into a butterfly.

Everyone breathed a sigh of relief. Seraphine glanced at Nilay. "Set course for the star Gliese 783 AB. Take us to Eleutheria."

"Course set for Gleise 783 AB," said Nilay.

Seraphine's smile faded when she looked at Ingli.

Untroubled, Ingli looked calmly back.

Seraphine turned away and looked at the Gisele. "Miss Ellestad, take us out of here."

Gisele closed her eyes, tuning into the frequency of the destination star. She sang another melody. The music was converted into light and projected out into space. A mandala of light appeared, a hyperspace wormhole, and the *Lethe* was drawn into it like a arrow fired from an ancient bow.

*　　*　　*

CHAPTER FOUR

Harmless

3142 A.D. — YEAR OF THE WATER HORSE

YELLOW DRAGON OF THE EARTH

THE FORBIDDEN PALACE — SOL/TERRA

It was a race.

Down the tall hill of green grass the children ran. They ran across a meadow and by tall trees. They sped past the monorail station. They ran until they come to a fence. Throwing themselves against the metal links, young Seraphine and the other children, including her best friend Katrina, caught their breath, letting excitement fill their lungs. Katrina shouted, "Look, Seraphine!"

The starship sat on the landing strip of the sky palace, its silver surface gleaming against the sun. The children laughed and pointed. Their eyes shone with the reflection of a million stars.

The starship's antigravity engines glowed and it took off. The children inclined their heads as it climbed high into the sky. Seraphine spoke. "One day, I'll fly away on a starship like that one!"

*　*　*

3234 A.D. — YEAR OF THE WOOD TIGER (PRESENT DAY)
HYPERSPACE WORMHOLE

Intruding upon Seraphine's memory, the door chime sounded, followed by Gisele's voice, "Captain DeVere?"

Inside her stateroom, Seraphine stood motionless by the window looking out into the blackness of the wormhole. Propelled by hypersails, the *Lethe* traveled through hyperspace. Stars were not visible, their light having shifted into the x-ray spectrum. The centralized bright glow of the universe left over from the Big Bang was all that remained.

Seraphine had changed into a loose, flowing white silk blouse with billowing sleeves. Over it, a fitted black leather waistcoat hugged her frame, its fine craftsmanship highlighted by intricate silver stitching that curled like tendrils of smoke. Her leggings, dark as night, slid into high leather boots polished to a brilliant shine. A crimson sash at her waist added a bold flash of color, its sharp red contrasting with the black and silver of her outfit. A belt, studded with brass and iron, secured both her laser pistol in a holster and a Vajra Thunderbolt baton. A red headscarf, wrapped around her forehead, kept her wild, untamed hair from falling into her eyes. Silver bracelets gleamed on her wrists, and a tricorn hat rested upon her desk.

"Come in."

Reflected in the glass window, Seraphine noticed the door open. Gisela stood there, silhouetted by the light in the passageway. Seraphine didn't bother to turn around. Her voice was cool, distant. "Yes?"

Gisele motioned towards the corner of the room where a delicate glass container sat, its contents a collection of origami stars, each folded with precision. There were hundreds of the little stars inside the glass. "Why do you keep it?"

Seraphine gave a brief, almost imperceptible shrug, her gaze never leaving the dark void. "I don't know."

Gisele took a step closer. Her voice was gentle but firm. "Take if from me, captain. It's a mistake to hold onto the past."

Seraphine didn't move, still lost in the darkness. She said nothing, and let the silence linger between them. After a long moment, she spoke, her voice quiet, distant. "Why are you here, Miss Ellestad?"

Gisele's reflection in the window shifted as she extended her hand, holding out a small data crystal. "Here's the report on Drake. He's a fine engineer and a crack shot."

Glancing over her shoulder, Seraphine pointed at the data reader.

Gisele moved forward with a fluid grace, crossing the room and inserting the crystal into the reader. A soft click echoed through the quiet room, followed by the soft whir of the machine as it powered on. A hologram flickered into existence above the reader, casting an eerie blue light across the desk. Sebastian Drake's face appeared, etched in electric light, his features sharp and unreadable, accompanied by a host of detailed statistics.

Seraphine gave the data a cursory review. She didn't need it. She met Gisele's gaze. "What do you think?"

Gisele tilted her head slightly, considering. She studied the hologram, her lips parting slightly. "There's something about him that's rather alluring."

The word hung there between them, like the aroma of something long forgotten. Seraphine's lips curled into a faint smirk, but the expression was fleeting. She turned fully to face Gisele. "Has he made any advances?"

Gisele's silence stretched between them like a taut wire. She crossed her arms. Her eyes, once so calculating, softened with uncertainty.

Seraphine tilted her head. "What is it, Sela?"

Gisele uncrossed her arms slowly. "By all what's holy and unholy, he's too perfect. I think he's hiding something."

Seraphine raised her eyebrows. "What could he hide?"

Gisele shrugged off the question. "The medical bot won't do much for him. If Galen were here—"

"Galen is dead," Seraphine interrupted, her voice cold. "But a healer can't give him what he needs."

Gisele looked up at the hologram of Drake. "He simply wants his memories back."

Seraphine turned her back on Gisele, her fingers grazing the crystal that still lay in the reader. She withdrew it and the hologram winked out. She held the crystal between her fingers as though it were something fragile. "The past is dead," she said, her voice distant. "Sebastian should think about the future."

Gisele nodded and moved toward the door.

Seraphine glanced at her before she went out. "Thank you for this."

A faint smile touched Gisele's lips.

The door opened and closed, leaving Seraphine alone. She looked at the crystal, lost in thought. *I wish I could forget all that I have done.* Her mind drifted back to the girl, Ingli. Seraphine closed her eyes, wishing the blackness outside would swallow her up into

67

forgetfulness.

The communicator chimed.

When she opened her eyes, Seraphine saw that the darkness outside had been replaced by a field of stars. She waved her hand and a hologram of Christian appeared. "Yes, Mr. Thiessen?"

Christian gave his report. "I have pleasure in saying, captain, that we have emerged from the wormhole and have arrived at Gliese 783 AB. We're retracting the hypersails. I gave the order for all hands to make sail as soon as Sela is finished tuning the solar sails."

Seraphine sighed in relief. The journey was almost over. "Thank you, Christian. I'll be there in a moment."

"Shall I unlock the door to Ingli's cabin?"

The thought of the girl walking around the *Lethe* disturbed her more than she wanted to admit. "No."

Christian's didn't understand Seraphine's reticence. "I understand how you want to prevent ill consequences from so dangerous an instrument of division and quarrel, captain. But do we really need to lock her up?"

A smile touched her lips. "You're attracted to her."

"She saved our lives."

"True enough." Seraphine wondered what to do with such a dangerous girl. "Follow my orders, Mr. Thiessen. Keep her away from the crew."

His sigh of disappointment was audible. "Very well."

*　*　*

BLACK TORTOISE OF THE NORTH
GLIESE 783 AB / ELEUTHERIA

Gisele stood at the bow of the *Lethe*, inside the fo'c'sle. A piano occupied the center of the room, its polished wood reflecting the dim light from the stars outside. She gazed through the viewport, where the cosmos unfolded like a dark velvet sea, dotted with a thousand silent embers. Ahead, two stars came into view: one orange and bright, the other red, an elusive ember in the dark—silent, waiting for the right moment to strike, just out of reach.

The stillness was disturbed by the sound of the door. Sebastian entered, a bee drawn to honey. His voice was quiet, like a whisper from the edge of a dream. "What is this place?"

Gisele looked at Drake. "We're at the bow of the starship. I come here sometimes, to look at the stars, and to sing."

Sebastian moved closer and he came up behind her. With a tender hand, he reached out and brushed a strand of hair from her face.

Startled, Gisele stepped away, her fingers brushing the edge of the piano. She moved around it, a quiet dance in the space between them.

Sebastian's gaze never left her, his eyes hungry. He leaned for-

69

ward with a smile on his lips. "Play me something."

After a moment's hesitation, Gisele sat down at the piano. "All right."

Her fingers began to move, the delicate music unfolding from the piano in a swift cascade of sound. The first note, clear and precise, floated into the room, followed by the next, and the next, each one adding to a swirling tapestry of melody, each passage weaving in and out like the ebbing tide of the sea. The music was elegant and yet playful, a lively sonata that seemed to lift the air around them.

Sebastian stood, transfixed, his eyes wide. The piece unfolded like a story, its movement rapid and thrilling, the harmonic shifts like a gentle breeze that tugged at his chest. As the final note faded into the silence of the room, he remained frozen, caught between awe and disbelief. "I've never heard music like this," he murmured. His words were a reverent whisper, as if he had just witnessed a miracle too beautiful to comprehend.

Gisele giggled. "Of course not. You've no memories."

"No, I have never heard anything like this," he said. "I would know. Let me see your hands."

Gisele showed her hands to him and he took them into his.

His words were full of wonder. "You have touched the mind of God with these hands. They're magic."

Gisele pulled her hands away from him. "My hands aren't

magic, but I am a starsinger."

"What does a starsinger do?"

Gisele played another tune on the piano as she spoke. "Each star has a unique frequency, like a fingerprint. When I tune into the frequency of a star with my intuition, I search for the quantum point in spacetime with the potential to manifest a wormhole. Potentiality becomes actuality and my song turns into light. A doorway to hyperspace will open, propelling us to our destination."

"You can hear the dynamic spheres of the universe."

"I listen to them, yes," she said. "You know, a thousand years ago during the Dark Ages of Science, people thought that spirituality and technology were two separate things. They rejected divine love, the true source of everything in the universe. Hundreds of millions of people died in their endless wars. Humanity lived in perpetual slavery."

Sebastian strolled over to her side. He began to caress her, so gently that she hardly noticed at first. "Why did you choose this life?"

"I fell in love with a pirate and then I fell in love with the life he led. He was free."

"Yes," he agreed. "A pirate's life is a good life. If you're able to take something, you deserve to have it. What happened to him?"

Suddenly aware of the caresses, she stood up, shaking him off.

The music stopped and silence filled the room. "He was murdered."

"Why?"

Gisele walked over to the window. "My previous captain wanted me in his bed. So, he arranged for an accident," she said. "When I learned of what he'd done, I tried to kill him."

"So now you serve on this starship, the Lethe."

"Yes," she said. Gisele thought of the captain and spoke without thinking. "Seraphine DeVere is a lost soul, like me."

"Has the captain lost someone too?"

Gisele didn't answer.

*   *   *

Christian stepped up to the door of Ingli's cabin. The sentry robot, a sleek, metallic sentinel, floated beside the door, silent and watchful, its sensors trained on him with unblinking efficiency. Christian's threw an irritated glance at the machine. The thing was always there, always watching. His hand hovered, hesitating, and then he knocked on the door with a quick, sharp rap.

Inside, the muffled sound of Ingli's sobs seeped through the walls, each one a quiet lament, a soft surrender to grief. Christian's jaw tightened, the sound scraping against his nerves.

When he opened the door, the sight that met him was disheartening. The cabin was small, cramped, almost suffocating, its walls closing in on her like a prison. Ingli sat hunched on the edge of the bed, her knees drawn tightly to her chest, her arms wrapped around them. Her face was a portrait of the despair. Her eyes were hollow with sorrow, her cheeks streaked with the remnants of her tears. Christian took a step inside, but found himself at a loss for words. He only knew that the sound of her weeping was unbearable.

Ingli wiped her eyes and gave him a tentative smile.

*   *   *

Ingli let Christian take her hand and he escorted her onto the star deck. Through the transparent force field above them, the stars shimmered like distant jewels. Ingli gazed at them, feeling the vast silence of the universe settle around her.

A distant melody floated down, pulling her attention upward. She noticed that some of the crew had climbed into the rigging. Christian spoke quietly, "They're called star riggers. They sing soft melodies to fine-tune the solar sails."

Christian led her to the crew lounge below decks, a quiet sanctuary at the aft of the *Lethe*. Inside, the lounge was empty. Ignoring the robot slave working behind the bar, Christian went over to the galley and prepared sandwiches and cold drinks.

When he brought the meal over and sat down, a smile tugged at her lips. It was small, almost imperceptible, but it was there. She hadn't expected this—kindness from a human, unasked for, unprompted. In truth, she wasn't sure what she had expected, but it certainly hadn't been this. The quiet simplicity of the moment caught her off guard, and for a brief moment, she wondered if she could let her guard down, just for a little while.

As they ate, the soft whir of the sentry robot broke the silence. Its polished metal surface reflected the muted lights in the room. It hovered nearby—silent, watchful, its presence as unyielding as ever. A guardian that never quite allowed her to be alone.

Ingli glared at the robot, the unsettling sense of being watched creeping back in. She turned her gaze back toward Christian, curiosity flickering across her face. "What is that object?"

Christian glanced down as his weapon, his fingers curling instinctively around the cool grip. "This? It's my sidearm."

Ingli touched the translator earring and frowned. "I do not understand your words."

Christian chuckled. "It's a weapon. A laser pistol."

Ingli's brow furrowed, her expression shifting to something between wonder and unease. "How does it work?"

Christian's movements were fluid, practiced, as he drew the pistol from its holster in one smooth motion. He pointed it at the wall. "You aim it at someone and then pull this trigger. A pulse of energized photons, light, will come out of the barrel and will streak towards the target. The hot light will burn whatever it strikes."

Wrinkling her face in revulsion, Ingli recoiled. "It is used for killing another?"

He met her gaze, the weight of his words heavy in the silence between them. "Yes."

Ingli tilted her head, a strange curiosity in her eyes. "Why would you ever want to do such a thing?"

Christian's shoulders shifted in a casual shrug. "Sometimes, it's necessary."

A dark smile crept into Ingli's face, her expression playful, almost childlike. But beneath it lurked an unfamiliar edge. "Point your laser pistol at your head."

Christian hesitated only a fraction of a second before the command settled into his mind. His fingers moved without resistance, lifting the cold barrel of the laser pistol to his temple.

Surprise mingled with a thought: *They will do anything.* Ingli's gaze sharpened, and a smile touched her lips, though she wasn't sure why. It felt like something playful, but distant, unsettling. She giggled softly, as she felt a strange rush, like a child playing with a dangerous toy. "Are you necessary?"

Before either one could say another word, Gisele walked in, stopped, and put her hands on her hips. "What are you doing?"

Seeming to come out of a trance, Christian shook his head and reholstered the weapon. He shrugged. "Just showing Ingli around."

Ingli spoke to him in a low voice, "You should go."

He got up and went out.

The sentry robot remained with Ingli.

Gisele glared at the robot. "What a useless piece of mechanical junk."

Ingli looked at Sela curiously but didn't say anything.

Gisele looked into Ingli's eyes. "You're not harmless at all, are you?"

Rather than replying, Ingli said, "Sebastian told me of your past. I am sorry for what happened to you."

Gisele crossed her arms. "I'll have my revenge some day."

Ingli touched her translator earring again and shook her head. "My language does not have this word. What is revenge?"

"Getting even. Retribution. Settling old scores."

"What do you derive from such actions?"

"Satisfaction, that's what."

Ingli's face turned from curiosity to sadness.

Gisele laughed out loud. "You don't know nothing."

Ingli remained silent.

Gisele stepped close to Ingli and lowered her voice. "Listen, you stay away from members of this crew, savvy?"

Ingli nodded. Sela glared at the sentry robot again and walked out of the room.

* * *

The *Lethe* sailed towards the water world, Eleutheria. Though two stars hung in the sky, it was the K3V star that provided most of the planet's illumination, while the red star remained a mere whisper of light in the vast, shadowed sky. The corsair retracted its solar sails and its masts just before it dropped down into the atmosphere of the planet for a landing. The world was covered with thousands of islands. The *Lethe* descended to the largest one of these where a city overlooked the ocean.

On the poop deck, Christian, sat at a console. Sebastian and Gisele were there, too, watching a holographic images of their approach to the planet. Ingli sat next to the hovering sentry robot.

On the main deck below a flight of stairs, Christian heard the sound of the door to Seraphine's cabin open and close. He heard Seraphine as she walked by the helmsman at the wheel and came up the flight of stairs to the poop deck.

The captain paused at the entrance for a moment. Her eyes touched Christian's for a moment. He could feel her displeasure, but before he could say anything the captain turned away. With a disapproving glance at Ingli, the captain sat down in the command chair without a word. Christian withheld a grin.

The hologram displayed the water world as it rushed by underneath them. One island gradually filled the hologram, revealing a port city. Christian looked over at Ingli. "New Kingston. The party town of the Imperium. There's a tavern for every ten residents."

"Tell me more of this world," said Ingli.

He said, "The planet is called, Eleutheria. It means, "Freedom.""

"I do not understand this word," said Ingli. "What is freedom?"

Gisele laughed. "How can you not know what freedom is?"

Dozens of starships floated on the bay of New Kingston. Propelled by antigravity, the hull of the *Lethe* reshaped itself into a boat and it gently landed in the water. Wood masts were raised over the main deck and sails were put up by robot slaves. The starship transformed into a sailing vessel and headed into the harbor.

Christian shut down the antigravity engines.

Seraphine glanced at Sebastian. "I'll escort our passengers out."

Sebastian and Ingli got up and followed Seraphine down the stairs to the quarterdeck. As they went out, Christian found himself unable to look away from the captain. Her beauty was captivating. Gisele hovered by the stairway leading down to the quarterdeck. Just as he began to go by, she grabbed him and threw him against the railing. Drawing a knife, she placed it against his throat.

Her words were full of fury. "Your life is a quest for impossible things, Christian. Like trying to take a rainbow out of the sky and place it under a glass."

"What are you talking about?"

"Love creates monsters," she said. "You think you can keep it a secret, but I see what's in your eyes. Don't ever break her heart."

Furious, he glared at Gisele. "Are you finished?"

Gisele sliced his cheek open with the knife. "Now I am. Savvy?"

She let go of him but kept her her knife handy.

"Death and damnation!" Christian wiped blood off his cheek. "Why protect her?"

"You're the quartermaster, aren't you? Next in line for command. I don't want anything happening to the captain," said Gisele. "I'm tired of serving men."

Christian glared at her. "I seem to remember you leaving us high and dry on that last raid. To desert a ship or its crew in battle is against our code. I wonder why the captain didn't execute you for running away?"

"I was following orders."

"Were you?"

"I came back for you, didn't I?" Gisele stepped back from him. "You don't remember what I did for you at all, do you?"

Christian walked over to a first aid kit and withdrew a small wand. Turning it on, he moved it over his face and the wound was healed instantly. " I don't know what you're talking about."

Gisele put the knife away. "I save your life and you don't even notice it! That Ingli truly is an enchantress. Stay away from her."

"I don't have to listen to you." He pushed past her and went down the stairs.

* * *

The airlock opened and a rush of warm air came into the gun deck. There was a scent of seawater in the air. Outside, there were dozens of starships anchored in the harbor next to normal sailing ships. Seraphine and Ingli stood in the airlock with Sebastian behind. The brighter of the two stars that warmed the planet was going down. Warm seawater lapped the hull of the *Lethe*.

Seraphine turned to look at Ingli. "Thank you for saving our lives."

A shadow of a smile touched Ingli's lips.

Seraphine's eyes turned cold. "I don't know where you got this but there's no way it belongs to you." She grabbed the medallion that hung around Ingli's neck and pulled it off.

"Now, get off my ship!" Seraphine shoved Ingli out of the airlock and the girl fell into the water of the bay with a shriek.

Sebastian was incredulous. "How could you?"

Seraphine watched Ingli swim away from the *Lethe*. "Nothing I do compares to what I have done."

* * *

CHAPTER FIVE
The Hunter

BLACK TORTOISE OF THE NORTH

HD 173818 / TAUTHE

Forty-six and a half light years from Sol, an immense starship, *The Royal Sovereign*, a ship 'o the line battleship, cut its way through the ruins of a shattered fleet. The flagship of the 10th Legion sailed through the wreckage, its hull gleaming in the void, flanked by a hundred surviving man 'o war cruisers and a host of sloop 'o war destroyers. Yet beyond them, the bulk of the legion lay in smoldering ruins, scattered across the cold abyss, burning silently in the vacuum. Fighter wings darted and weaved through the debris fields, patrolling the wreckage. The 10th Legion had suffered a crushing defeat, its might all but eradicated.

The rhythmic beat of polished boots resounded over the polished star deck of *The Royal Sovereign*, each step measured, purposeful. A cadre of officers marched in precise formation, led by Magister Militum Walter Ernsting, the Imperium's supreme military commander. Their faces were grim, their eyes like flint. A sixteen-pointed Imperial Star gleamed from the chest of each officer, an unspoken declaration of their loyalty to the Imperium. They came up a flight of stairs to the poop deck.

Consul Leopold Voss, First Citizen of the Imperium, stood at the edge of *The Royal Sovereign's* command deck, his sharp eyes scanning the chaos that unfolded before him. The stars beyond were a glittering ocean of cold, distant light, but his focus was fixed on the scene in front of him. In his hand, he gripped the Vajra Thunderbolt baton—its polished surface glinting like a weapon forged by the gods themselves. The weight of it was not just symbolic, it was the weight of destiny, of countless lives shaped by his command.

Around him, officers moved with practices precision, their faces etched with the solemnity of their duty. The hum of the starship's operations filled the air as their eyes flicked across the readouts, each officer immersed in the silent rhythm of war.

Through the transparent force field that shielded the star deck, Leopold watched as the remains of the 10th Legion drifted through the blackness. Devastation, in all its silent glory, spread before him—starships broken, their wreckage spinning like the scattered bones of a fallen beast. He could not look away. The sight stirred something primal in him, something more than mere leadership. It was the resolve of a conqueror who had seen countless battles, yet never grew numb to the price of victory.

Suddenly, a flash—bright, furious—erupted in the distance. A starship detonated, its fiery death casting a fleeting brilliance that illuminated the void. For an instant, the darkness was gone, devoured by the raw, searing light. But it did not last. The brilliance faded, like the dying gasp of a fallen titan, leaving only the cold, eternal darkness once more.

The casualty reports came in, relentless, like the ticking of a countdown. Each number weighed heavy on the heart—each was a testament to the blood spilled in the name of the Imperium. Yet Leopold did not flinch. He had faced worse. He had known the cost of empire long before this moment. The stars would not care about the lives lost here. Only the strength of his will mattered. He turned sharply toward the communication station as Ernsting and a cadre of officers arrived, snapping to attention at his presence. "Bring the rest of te 10th Legion to our position," Leopold commanded, his voice cold but firm.

Ernsting hesitated for a moment, his brow furrowing slightly.

"The order has already been given, Consul Voss."

Leopold's lips curled into the faintest of smiles. "Very good." He clasped the Vajra Thunderbolt baton with both hands behind his back, the weapon now an extension of his will. His boots clicked against the deck as he paced slowly in front of the officers, his gaze unwavering. "I know what you're thinking Ernsting. These aliens have a high level of technology but they don't have the mental capacity to use it. They're little more than mongrel animals."

"Yes, sir," agreed Ernsting, his tone cold, full of disdain. "They are indeed miserable creatures. If only more of our starships had been at the battle. The shortage of sunstones was at a critical level when we began our attack on Tauthe."

Leopold came to a sudden halt in front of the officers, his posture rigid. The silence that followed was thick with the weight of loss, yet it did not daunt him. His gaze remained fixed ahead. After a long drawn out moment, he spoke, his voice sharp and commanding. "We'll make do." The words were not a suggestion, they were a declaration, as absolute as the laws of nature. He turned, his eyes scanning the group. "We always triumph in the end."

A smile tugged at the corner of his mouth. "Victory is my destiny."

Before Ernsting could respond, one of the communication officers interrupted. "Sir, a high priority message has arrived through the hyperspace communications network from the planet Bijon Bleu."

The officer's words drew Leopold's attention. The hyperspace communication crystals were the only way for instant communication across the galaxy. The ancient artifacts had been discovered a hundred years ago, but there were only a few dozen of them. Their existence was top secret. Only proconsuls from the provinces were permitted to use them, and a few others. Everyone else in the Imperium had to make due with robot courier drones that delivered communication data packets to the network nodes inside star systems. If the sender was using the rare communication crystals, the message must have been important.

Ernsting put his hands behind his back. "Put it on the viewer."

Leopold shook his head. "No, I'll take it in my office. Carry on with the redeployment."

Leopold left the poop deck and descended a flight of stairs to the quarterdeck. He walked by the wheelhouse and made his way aft, heading for his private office. Windows in his office framed the chaos of the wrecked legion out there, drifting, broken. He sat down and let out a long sigh, the burden of leadership heavy on his shoulders. With a simple gesture, the communication channel came to life. The image of the sixteen-pointed Imperial Star on the viewscreen was replaced by the face of Tribune Dominic Fontaine.

Behind the officer, the blue planet Bijon Bleu loomed large. Leopold crossed his arms. "What is it, Tribune?"

Although he looked nervous, Dominic smiled at Consul Voss. "Greetings, citizen. I have found the pirate captain responsible for our troubles. Seraphine DeVere."

A foggy memory tugged at Leopold. "I know that name."

"Yes, sir," said Dominic. "She once served in the military as a Watcher. She was the captain of the Brandywine, a scout ship exploring the frontiers of the Imperium. She —"

"Where is she now?"

Dominic swallowed hard. "We had captured her, sir, but she's managed to escape."

One of the starships of the legion exploded. The silent flash of light blinded Leopold for a moment, but the window automatically turned black. He glanced outside and then turned back to Dominic, fury in his voice. "These pirates are destroying our ability to pacify inferior species on the frontier. Find that pirate, Tribune. I want her. Dead or alive."

"Yes, sir."

Leopold's hand hovered over the control panel, assuming the communication was at an end, but something in Dominic's expression told him otherwise. The Tribune hesitated, as if weighing his next words. Leopold's gaze sharpened. "What else?"

Dominic's voice came, low and strained, laced with unmistakable tension. "That alien we were interrogating has escaped." He paused, his eyes flicking to the side as if reluctant to say more. "We think the pirate helped her to get away."

A chill slithered down Leopold's spine, freezing the blood in his veins. His mind, momentarily paralyzed, struggled to grasp the enormity of the situation. The fire that had burned inside him now turned to ice, the heat of anger replaced by a creeping dread. He rose from his seat, his voice barely more than a whisper, as though the words themselves might unleash something terrible. "Has she found Archon?"

Dominic's eyes met his, solemn. "There's no way to know, sir."

Leopold's gaze narrowed. He leaned forward slightly, his mind racing. "Do you still believe the alien intends to use a weapon from Archon against earth?"

Dominic didn't hesitate. "There is no doubt of that, sir. We destroyed her world."

The words struck Leopold like a sudden clash of steel. He sank back into his chair, his posture still commanding, though a fire flickered in his eyes. After a moment, he spoke again, his voice laced with a quiet, dangerous curiosity. "You're an enhanced human, are you not?"

Dominic straightened, his posture sharp. "Yes sir. Compared

to pure strains, I'm faster, stronger —"

"It is a wonder that the prisoners managed to escape from your care, Tribune."

Dominic sell silent.

Leopold's words were like fire. "Put your superior intellect to work, Tribune. I'm promoting you to Legatus Legionis. I'm giving you command of the 9th Legion, which is stationed at Bijon Bleu. I am also authorizing the transfer of the hyperspace communication crystal of Bijon Bleu to your starship. I want regular reports. All of the Imperium's resources are at your disposal. Find the pirate, Seraphine DeVere and the alien."

Dominic bowed. "It shall be done, sir."

* * *

3132 A.D. — YEAR OF THE WATER MONKEY
(102 YEARS AGO)
YELLOW DRAGON OF THE EARTH
THE FORBIDDEN PALACE — SOL / TERRA

Darkness. A cold wind blew. The sounds of the burning city rose above the wind. A young girl called out in a weak voice, "Mommy, mommy, I want some apple juice."

The little girl, Seraphine, was just six years old. She lay on the ground with a cut on her forehead. She opened her eyes and rose to a sitting position, clutching a pink unicorn stuffed animal. Blood dripped into her face. A glimmer of sunlight rose above the horizon, throwing light over the landscape. She was surrounded by the ruins of a dead city. Fires were everywhere. Smoke rose up into the sky.

* * *

3234 A.D. — YEAR OF THE WOOD TIGER (PRESENT DAY)
BLACK TORTOISE OF THE NORTH
GLIESE 783 AB / ELEUTHERIA

"Don't touch that!"

Sunset was visible through the stern windows of Seraphine's stateroom aboard the *Lethe*. Sebastian Drake stood in front of her desk. He was reaching for a pink unicorn stuffed animal.

Sebastian pulled his hand back. "Oh, sorry. Is it something special?"

Ignoring his question, Seraphine pointed to a paper on the desk. "If you agree on certain articles of our code, which are put down in writing, then you can join my crew." She pushed the paper towards him. "Every person shall obey my civil commands. If anyone runs away in battle or keeps any secret from us, they shall be marooned or shot. Anyone striking another crew member shall be marooned or put to death. The code is all written down there." She paused for a moment before continuing. "We're not the most successful pirate crew, but the Lethe has the best stealth technology in the Imperium."

89

Seraphine's gaze fell upon him, and she couldn't help but feel a chill crawl across her skin. Sebastian Drake stood before her, a figure both haunting and strange—an enigma wrapped in the shadow of his own forgotten past. His features were sharp, almost sculptural, with a hollow, angular jawline that seemed to cut through the dim light of the room. His skin was pale, unnaturally so, as though the warmth of life itself had been drained from him. In his eyes, there was a cold, calculating emptiness, the unmistakable gaze of a predator waiting patiently in the shadows, ever-hungry, ever-watchful. Beneath his eyes, the shadow of a beard lingered. His hair, long and black, cascaded over his shoulders in a wild, untamed tangle, as though the very winds of oblivion had sculpted it into a snarled mass of shadows. Seraphine shuddered involuntarily. There was something disturbingly familiar about him, something that spoke not of humanity but of something *other*, a being of hunger and darkness, whose past had been buried—or torn away—leaving only the raw, insatiable core of a creature lost in the void of its own forgotten history. Sebastian's words snapped her out of her reverie. "Will I remember your code?" he asked. "I can't recall anything else in my life."

Seraphine leaned back in her chair, looking out the window at New Kingston harbor. The star Gliese 783 had gone down, and the city lights from the casinos, bars and entertainment venues were coming on, lighting up the sky. It was a world where one could escape the past. She whispered, "How I envy you."

Sebastian didn't respond. He had a blank expression on his face. She wondered if he was thinking anything at all. "Sign it," she said. "You can read it again and again if you want."

Sebastian nodded, picked up a pen and signed it.

She took the paper and gave him a copy.

He folded the paper up carefully and put it in his pocket.

Seraphine wondered what it would be like to have no memories. "Just one more thing, she said. "Why do you want to join my crew?"

Sebastian smiled. "I am a hunter, captain."

He's the perfect pirate. She resisted an impulse to smile at him. "Who are you hunting?"

Bewilderment flickered across his face. "I don't know."

Seraphine stared at him for a moment, pondering. *How did the Imperium erase his memories? What happened to him?* She felt a strange affinity for the man. He was so lost, and yet, he was in command of some kind of dark aura. As if a powerful spiritual being stood before her, shrouded in mystery. Whether an angel or devil, she couldn't tell.

She stood up and offered him her hand. "Welcome to the Lethe."

Sebastian shook her hand. Bewilderment was replaced with a smile, a purpose.

He opened the door and went out. Seraphine saw Christian standing just outside, looking like he had something to say. *How cute.* She waved him in and sat down in her chair again. "I'm going over to the Flying Dragon to have a talk with Bartacus."

Christian's face wore that insufferable, concerned look again. *Always trying to protect me, but we don't ever dance to the same tune, do we?* Resisting an urge to roll her eyes, she let out a loud sigh. "What now?"

He crossed his arms, looking rather like a dog with a bone he couldn't quite bury. "I'm concerned about your choice of targets. Military supply ships are too well guarded."

"We did all right."

"We were lucky," he shot back. "You know, all of the pirates in history had a bad end."

Seraphine chuckled and leaned back in her chair, stretching like a cat."Oh, but don't you just love a good tragedy, Christian?" She picked up a dagger on her desk and started playing with it. "Ching Shih was a successful pirate."

"Who?"

Putting the knife down, Seraphine waved her hand over a reader and a hologram of a fierce looking Chinese woman materialized in front of them. "Ching Shih. Two thousand years ago, she commanded an immense fleet of ships. She challenged the empires of her time." Seraphine leaned forward onto her arms. "Here's the best part—she was never defeated."

Christian raised an eyebrow. "What makes you think you're as good as she was?"

Seraphine smiled, her eyes glinting with mischief.

* * *

AZURE DRAGON OF THE EAST
HD 172051 / BIJON BLEU

Dominic Fontaine walked out onto the quarterdeck of the *Persephone*, followed by Inanna. Several crew members sat at consoles. A dozen bounty hunters awaited his arrival. An attractive, solemn young woman with a sober look in her eyes, was among them. The woman had an antique suit of battle armor which appeared to have been modified. *Upgraded*, he realized. Dominic recognized that she was from an older era, before the centurions. She was a Knight of the Republic. *How many times have you used an age regression chamber? How old are you?*

Dominic couldn't use age regression chambers to extend his lifespan because he had chosen to become an enhanced human. He had sacrificed a long lifespan for superior abilities. He sought greatness. He was one of the elites now.

Inanna walked through the group of bounty hunters, admiring each one in turn. She halted in front of the knight. "You're a Champion, are you not?"

The woman nodded.

Recognition flashed in Dominic's mind as he realized the woman wasn't just a simple bounty hunter. The name hung in the air—*Champion*. The Champion Games were the most popular sport in the Imperium, a brutal spectacle that captivated millions. Bounty hunters, all competing for an annual grand prize, were televised as they hunted down the most dangerous criminals in the Imperium. It was a deadly mix of the ancient gladiatorial games and the hunt, where only the strongest, the smartest, and the most ruthless survived. A flicker of doubt crept into his mind. Champions were known for putting on a show for the crowd. They were often more focused on spectacle than actually catching their prey.

At a nod from Dominic, Inanna waved a hand and a hologram of Seraphine, wearing a white imperial uniform, appeared before them.

Dominic pointed at the hologram. "This is your target. Seraphine DeVere. You shall be well paid when you return her to me, unharmed. I want her alive at all costs." He paused for a moment before continuing. "One more thing, watch out for imperial assassins. You're not the only ones hunting her."

The Champion Knight spoke, "A Pure Strain! Why are we hunting a citizen?"

Dominic met her gaze. "What's your name?"

"I am Chevaliere Celestine Ney from Ra'iatea."

Dominic smiled at the knight. "DeVere is a legitimate target. The order comes from Consul Leopold Voss himself. After DeVere has been delivered to me, I shall escort her to the Forbidden World where she will stand trial for piracy and treason."

Celesting laughed. "A trial on earth? The people will never condemn her to death."

"Nevertheless, she will stand trial, alive," he said. "DeVere was last seen traveling with these three. The last one appears human, but she is an alien."

Holograms of Christian Thiessen, Sebastian Drake and Inglina Nivienne appeared.

Celestine looked at Sebastian and smiled.

The other bounty hunters downloaded the information on their targets. One of the bounty hunters, a man with red hair and a beard, mumbled, "I didn't know there were any aliens that looked like us."

Inanna halted next to the man. "They are quite rare," she said. "This one is an exile, so feel free to shoot her if you can."

Inanna handed out golden Vajra Thunderbolt batons as Dominic continued. "As bounty hunters and Free Imperial Knights you have limited authority, but this imperial warrant shall grant you full access to all resources within the Imperium."

His gaze shifted to Celestine. In that moment, he realized he had just given her competitors the same authority held by the Champions—*more* authority, in fact. She didn't react at all. *Perhaps she enjoys the competition.*

Celestine activated the golden thunderbolt. In an instant, the weapon shifted, reshaping itself into a spear encased in shimmering ice. The air around her grew colder, her breath crystallizing into fog. She moved with fluid grace, the ice spear flashing as she waved it through the air. Beneath her feet, the floor of the starship began to freeze, a layer of frost spreading outward in perfect, crystalline patterns. A smile tugged at the corners of her lips, a look of quiet satisfaction as she deactivated the thunderbolt. The ice spear retracted smoothly into its baton form, the chill receding as quickly as it had come.

Dominic couldn't help but feel a spark of awe, his admiration hidden beneath his usual stoic expression. Celestine was a force unto herself—effortless, precise, and unpredictable.

Dominic and Inanna exchanged a look of satisfaction.

* * *

BLACK TORTOISE OF THE NORTH
GLIESE 783 AB / ELEUTHERIA

A fine morning dawned on Eleutheria. Starships floated in the waters of the bay while the two suns climbed high into the sky. Seraphine approached one of the starships, the *Flying Dragon*. Just as she stepped onto the pier where it was moored, several police units arrived in hovercars, their engines humming ominously as the glided to a halt. She grinned. *Oh, what fun, they've come to dance with the Devil.*

Seraphine sat down on the pier next to a small boy with a silver collar around his neck. Out of the corner of her eyes, she observed the police pass by, their hands gripping stun batons, oblivious to her presence here. *It looks like the game is over for Bart. Oh, well.* Seraphine leaned back on her hands and let her legs dangle over the water. The boy was throwing rocks at Phinians, the dolphin-like natives of the planet. The police went by and entered the *Flying Dragon* just as a stone hit a Phinian. The inferior alien let out a painful cry and dove underwater.

A frown tugged at her lips. Seraphine had no tolerance for petty cruelty, even if it was against inferiors. "Why are you hurting them?"

The boy was not more than ten years old. "Why wouldn't I?"

Glancing around, Seraphine noticed that all of the exits on the pier were blocked. "The natives of this planet, the Phinians, are under our guidance and protection. Don't be cruel."

The boy chuckled. "That's stupid."

Nonplussed, Seraphine was silent.

The boy looked up at her. "Oh, did I hurt your feelings? Sorry. But you are stupid. We need to show 'em who's boss."

He threw another rock, which struck a Phinian swimming by the pier.

Seraphine grumbled, "Sounds like Imperial propaganda."

"What's propaganda?"

"Tell me your name and I'll tell you what propaganda is."

"I'm Victor."

"No last name?"

"No, just Viktor."

Seraphine explained, "Propaganda is a lie the government tells you."

The sharp crack of a blaster ripped through the air from the *Flying Dragon*. Seraphine's eyes narrowed, but the amusement on her face never faltered. The police stormed off the starship, Black Bartacus between them, all cuffs and scowls. Their boots thudded on the pier, heavy with purpose, as they started checking the rest of the crowd, eyes flicking over faces, measuring who might be trouble.

Seraphine tilted her head.

Viktor's voice cut through the moment, loud and insistent.

98

"You're a friend of Black Bartacus, aren't you?"

Seraphine shushed him.

"You are!"

Seraphine glanced over at an approaching police officer, his uniform stiff, his eyes darting between them like a man who wasn't sure if he was chasing a criminal or just a headache. She considered taking a dive into the ocean, disappearing into the dark water with a splash, but the thought didn't thrill her. There were better ways to play the game.

Viktor cracked a grin. "You want to get away from them? I can help."

So he wants to play. Seraphine whispered, "What do you want?"

Viktor touched the collar around his neck.

Though slavery was outlawed in the Imperium, some still practiced it, hidden in the shadows like a dirty little secret. The people involved in that sort of business were the worst kind. She hated them with every bone in her body. "Why not ask your parents to remove it?"

She knew the answer before he said it. "They're dead."

For a moment, her heart went out to him, a fleeting softness she rarely allowed herself to feel. She studied his face, sensing the vulnerability beneath his bravado. But then, a trace of mischief flickered in her eyes, and the moment passed. *Ah, a good deed now and then—just a little treat for me.* Seraphine nodded. "Very well. We have a bargain."

They shook hands. Seraphine whispered, "The next time I see you—"

A pair of police officers approached.

Viktor picked up a stone, stood up and threw it at a Phinian, striking it. The Phinian gave out a loud cry of pain. Viktor laughed out loud and picked up another stone.

"Hey, kid!"

He threw the rock at one of the officers, who recoiled to avoid it. Viktor ran away and the police chased after him.

Smiling, Seraphine used the distraction to slip away.

* * *

The *Lethe* sat in silence, a hulking shadow against the flickering lights of the distant city. The crew, lost in the temptations of the sprawling party town, had all but abandoned the starship to spend their earnings in the neon-lit streets. Yet, Sebastian remained, a solitary figure in his cabin, untouched by the allure of the city.

He stared at his reflection in the mirror, the face before him an unfamiliar blur. Each feature seemed to shift, as though the very image he sought to recognize was slipping through his fingers. The sterile white walls of his cabin offered no comfort, only a suffocating reminder of the hollow emptiness gnawing at the edges of his mind.

He reached out, fingers trembling, as though the reflection might offer him some kind of answer, some long-lost memory that would piece him together. His voice was barely a whisper, the word feeling foreign on his tongue. "Computer?"

"Yes?"

His voice was louder this time. "Search Eleutheria's communication matrix. Are there any messages for a Sebastian Drake?"

"No," said the computer. "However, there is an incoming call on an encrypted channel."

Sebastian's mind was clouded with doubt, confusion. An odd weight pressed against his thoughts. *An incoming call?* His gaze drifted to the control panel, where the blinking lights seemed to pulse in time with the beat of his own heart.

"Now?"

"Yes," came the computer's reply.

"Connect me."

A striking woman materialized in the holographic display. Her black hair was styled in a sharp wedge cut, framing her face with precision. She carried herself with a dignity that bordered on the regal, her presence exuding an unmistakable aristocratic grace. Her eyes, an unsettling shade of blue, pierced the dim light of the cabin with a hungry intensity. The look in her eyes was strangely familiar. *We are the same, you and me*, he thought.

101

A grin slipped into her face. "Hello, Drake."

The name seemed familiar, but it took a moment for him to piece it together. *My name is Sebastian Drake.* He swallowed the bitter taste of confusion. "Who are you?" The rest of his words tumbled out, more a reflex than a question. "How? What do you want?"

She laughed, low and smooth. "Cut the jokes, Drake. How'd you like to be rich?"

Sebastian stared at the hologram, not answering.

"Got your attention did I?" she teased, her voice soft with amusement. "I've always loved the look in your eyes when you smell blood in the water."

His hand grabbed the edge of the console, the cool metallic surface grounding him, though his thoughts remained clouded. "Tell me your name," he demanded, the words sharper than intended.

She shook her head, a hint of annoyance in her eyes. "Celestine," she replied, her tone dripping with mockery.

The name hung in the air, like a challenge, something both familiar and distant. A word came to his mind. *Champion.* She was a Champion. *Like me.* He relaxed somewhat. "What's the offer?"

Celestine leaned forward. She spoke in a low, conspiratorial tone. "Seraphine DeVere. She's worth a lot of money to the Imperium. Just tell me where to find her and I'll cut you in."

Sebastian smiled.

*   *   *

CHAPTER SIX
Crazy Alice

BLACK TORTOISE OF THE NORTH

GLIESE 783 AB / ELEUTHERIA

New Kingston was a city that never slept. The neon lights sliced through the night, illuminating bars, nightclubs, casinos, and other houses of ill repute. The city pulsed with a reckless energy, its streets teeming with tourists from every corner of the Imperium, all eager to indulge in its hedonistic promises. They had come to play on the greatest party planet in the Imperium.

High above, the magnificent palace stood bathed in the warm glow of the setting suns, casting long shadows over the sprawling city below. On one side, it overlooked the glittering expanse of New

Kingston. On the other, the dark ocean stretched endlessly into the horizon.

Inside the palace, Praefect William Parker sat at his ornate desk, its surface gleaming with polished mahogany and adorned with intricate brass inlays. The edges were carved with bold, neoclassical motifs—eagles and laurel wreaths. William's eyes were locked onto the holographic image of Gallows Point. A dozen pirate corpses swayed from the gibbets, their tales now nothing more than a brutal spectacle. Among them, Black Bartacus, once a name whispered in fear, was now a swinging corpse. William had always enjoyed using death as a stage to perform his dominance.

A camera drone hovered in front of him, silently watching and recording everything.

William didn't acknowledge the drone. He didn't need to. He was already aware of the angle, the lighting, the perception. Everything was carefully curated, even his most calculated silence. He was giving a speech, but every word, every pause, was part of a performance.

"Interstellar piracy," he began, drawing out the words, "has spread like the plague. Let these executions be a warning to all who seek such a despicable life." The phrasing was sharp, designed to sting. He was good at this, speaking with the confidence of someone who knew the game, who'd mastered the art of making people believe he was the solution.

"As a ruler of Eleutheria," he continued, his tone almost a touch self-congratulatory, "I've sentenced over two hundred pirates to death this year alone." He paused, letting the number settle in the air, an echo of his power.

"We must also dismantle the financial networks that make it possible to launder the money stemming from pirate activities." A promise, no doubt, a declaration for the future. A future where he reigned supreme. "Rest assured," he finished, his voice a shade cooler, "we shall eliminate piracy from the Imperium once and for all."

The camera light blinked off as the drone flew toward the exit, halting midair. A robot slave opened the door, allowing the drone to glide through. The slave followed, stepped out of the room, turned around, and shut the door, granting them some privacy.

William stood up and walked over to where Seraphine reclined on a couch.

Seraphine frowned, tossing a hyper-dimensional bag from one hand to the next like it was a toy. "So, tell me, why'd you execute Black Bartacus?"

William scowled. "He was too ambitious."

Seraphine looked outside at the city lights. Most of her crew were there, now, having their wealth drained away by rum, women and gambling. She closed her eyes, remembering the sight of Bartacus as he was dragged away in chains. "You know, they almost caught me," she said. "I was right in front of his starship when they took him."

William didn't even glance at her. His voice was smooth, dismissive, a practiced confidence. "Nonsense. You're too good."

Seraphine looked at the hologram of pirate corpses dangling from the gibbets. Hangings on Eleutheria were a regular occurrence. The bodies were placed inside the medieval cages and hung up for public display. She examined the current occupants. "I don't recognize the others," she said. "Who were they?"

The smile returned to his face and he held out his hand. "They were amateurs," he said. "Non-performers have the habit of getting caught on my planet."

Seraphine took his hand and they went out of the room. They made their way to a luxuriously appointed chamber. Decorated in the ancient Empire style of 19th century France, the imposing furniture was beautiful, but solemnity prevailed over comfort. Seraphine sat down on a burgundy mahogany sofa and looked out of the window at the ocean. The Empire clock on the mantelpiece chimed and she briefly admired a golden Eros statue plucking on a lyre. A servant entered with a silver tray. Seraphine noticed that it was not a robot slave, but an attractive woman. Seraphine and

William took drinks from the tray and he waved her away. Another woman entered and sat down on William's lap. She wrapped her arms around him and kissed him on the cheek.

William smiled. "The universe is abundant, my friend."

Seraphine presented the bag holding the sunstones to William, but he didn't take it.

He said, "I sense that you have sad news."

Seraphine nodded. "Galen is dead."

William's face darkened. "Galen was a great healer. I shall miss him."

Seraphine wondered how far his concerned act would go. He'd played the role of the caring leader for so long that it almost seemed genuine—almost. But she knew better. Beneath the surface, was a cold, calculating ambition that ran deeper than any facade of compassion. He was no longer the spiritual teacher she had once admired. In the past, he had been a figure of quiet wisdom, his presence calm and centered, like still water that reflected both the world around him and the depths of one's soul.

William's eyes drifted over to the bag in her hand. "Why are you doing this to them?

Sometimes she wondered why she continued to fight against the might of the Imperium. Her eyes drifted outside, where moonlight covered the ocean in silver. "Humanity has lost something," she said. "We've become monsters. I met this little boy today—"

"How old are you, Seraphine?"

Seraphine stopped talking. He wasn't listening to her anyway. "I am eleventy-one."

"One hundred and eleven years old," he said.

A holographic image of an individual's soul was made at a specific moment in time and was stored in a computer matrix. After a person had lived their life to a certain point, they could undergo age regression. In the process, a coma was induced and the person was placed in an age regression chamber. The holographic image of their soul was reintegrated with their body, and it was restored to the condition it was in at the moment in time it was created. The process was not without risks, however. There was always a chance that it would kill the person. The risk increased with each successive treatment until age regression was no longer practical. While this technology did not grant immortality, it had effectively increased the lifespan of humans. This technology didn't work on enhanced humans without killing them, however.

"How many times?" he asked.

"Twice," she said.

William sipped his drink, eyes fixed on her with that familiar, calculating gaze. "Did you know that our ancestors lived only a fraction as long as we do today?"

110

Before age regression treatments, a person could live nearly a century. "They didn't survive long, no."

William's lips curled into that smile. "The most fundamental value of society is survival."

"I know that."

The woman in his lap kissed him and whispered in his ear, but William didn't give in to the distraction. "So what troubles you?"

Seraphine looked outside at the dark ocean. She could hear the sounds of waves crashing across the beach. "If humans are truly superior, then why have we become so warlike?"

"A trillion people died in the Hymenopteran War," he said. "The bugs nuked every city on earth, and they hit most of our colonies, too."

"Yes, I was in Melbourne when it was destroyed."

William set his drink down. "Leopold Voss had to become ruthless to defeat our enemies," said William. "Every human being owes their life to him. He's the savior of humanity."

"He is."

William's eyes narrowed. "Yet, you fight against him."

She didn't answer immediately. Instead, she glanced at the Empire clock, the ticking sound filling the silence between them. "I just want it all to end."

William's smile faltered for a moment. "Continuing to attack supply ships will weaken the Imperium. This is the last military cargo that I will purchase from you."

Seraphine's eyes shifted back to his. "I'll double your share next time."

He raised his eyebrows, a small, knowing nod following. A man of principles—until money was involved. Never one to turn away a profit, he leaned forward and took the bag of sunstones out of Seraphine's hand. "Irresistible, as always."

* * *

The cold wrapped itself around Ingli like a ghostly ribbon, winding through her bones with quiet insistence. She trembled uncontrollably, shivering as she hugged her legs for warmth, though the chill seemed to settle deeper with every breath. Beneath the looming shadow of Gallows Point, she huddled against the rough-hewn stone, her thin dress soaked and clinging like a second skin. Wet strands of hair clung to her cheeks, veiling the silent tracks of her tears. She curled tighter, hoping the smallness of her body might trap what warmth remained, willing the dark to forget she was there.

Above her, the gibbets creaked in the wind, where a dozen corpses hung from steel cages, tainting the air with the stench of decay. Their faces were barely visible in the darkness, pale and slack, their eyes empty, staring into a world that had long since forgotten them. A nearby sign read: Pirates Be Warned!

A figure emerged from the shadows. An aquatic creature glided forward, his movements fluid and deliberate, like a shadow drifting over water. His skin, a mosaic of iridescent scales, shifted in color—deep teal and sapphire, the shades of the ocean's depths, catching the light with an almost hypnotic gleam. His eyes, bright and unfathomable, burned through the night like twin lanterns, their glow piercing the darkness with an eerie clarity, as though nothing could escape their gaze. He was tall, and despite the cold, there was a quiet warmth to him, an odd comfort that made her feel both drawn to him and wary. He stopped a few paces away, his dark eyes locked on hers.

He spoke with a strange blend of hisses and rasping sounds, but the translator earring she wore made his words clear. "Why do you sit, covered in water?"

Ingli froze, terrified. Had this creature come out of the sea, following her? She remained silent, hugging her knees and shivering in the cold.

The alien tilted his head slightly. "You're alone."

Ingli looked away, her heart pounding.

"I am Shtol," said the alien. He held out his hand. "Come."

The silence stretched, heavy with fear. *Maybe this stranger is not as cruel as the humans.*

Ingli hesitated, her body trembling. Slowly, she rose to her feet and took his hand. There was no turning back. She let him lead her away into the night.

* * *

A large mirror was mounted on the wall behind a grand mahogany bar. Seraphine and William enjoyed another glass of wine while gazing out at the city. The attractive woman in the Praefect's lap whispered in his ear, giggling. He gave her a kiss. "I'll meet up with you later."

The woman got up and left the chamber. Seraphine gulped her drink down. Her question came out as a playful challenge. "You have anything stronger?"

William barely glanced at her, his hand a casual flick towards the robot slave. The robot glided across the room, its gleaming chrome body reflecting the soft light of the bar. With a soft whirr, it slipped behind the counter with mechanical precision, its hands reaching out to gather a selection of liquor bottles. Each one was carefully arranged on a silver tray, a gleaming array of spirits, like stars lined up for a celestial dance. Without a word, it set the tray down in front of Seraphine. She picked a bottle, the glass clinking faintly as she poured herself another drink.

William's eyes lingered on her face. "Celebrating again?"

"What do you care?"

"So, you're just another tormented soul."

Seraphine laughed, downed the drink and poured another with a theatrical flourish. "Not just another tormented soul. I'm unique."

William stood up and went over to the window, looking down at the city below. Seraphine followed his movements, her eyes glinting with an unspoken amusement. After a moment of quiet reflection, he spoke again. "You call us monsters. You know, there are all kinds of people. Some are kind, noble beings—enlightened, even. Some are more selfish. Then there are the bad ones." He turned back to her, his tone a mixture of resignation and finality. "You can't change any of them."

Seraphine leaned back against the back of the burgundy couch, her fingers tracing the rim of her glass. "I can try."

He walked over to the bar and poured himself another drink. She watched his face in the mirror. It was full of doubt. "Frankly, I don't see you succeeding. But there's no harm in making a lot of money along the way, is there?"

Seraphine got up and walked over to the balcony. A cool breeze met her there, whipping a strand of hair across her face. She brushed it aside and looked down at New Kingston. The city was a sea of neon lights and flickering signs, casting long shadows across the ocean's surface. Seraphine leaned against the balcony, the cool stone railing pressing into her skin as she stared out over the bustling metropolis. The sounds of the city below filtered in faintly, the hum of hovercars, the occasional cheer from a distant nightclub, the quiet whisper of life in motion. She raised her glass, swirling the amber liquid before taking a long sip, savoring the burn that trickled down her throat. "You're a clever one, William. Everyone believes you're trying to eliminate piracy. If the truth were known—"

Her words died down to silence.

He was staring at her in the mirror. "What's that around your neck?"

Seraphine's hand fell to Ingli's medallion instinctively. "This? I took it from an alien. It's made out of a strange metal."

William crossed the room toward her, the soft click of his boots against the marble floor the only sound. Stepping out onto the balcony, he picked up the medallion from around her neck, lifting it slightly above her chest. Moonlight caught the intricate geometric patterns. "This is an extremely rare metal. It came from Archon."

"The mythical world of the ancients?" Seraphine's voice held a trace of mockery, her eyebrows raised.

"Indeed." William's fingers traced the medallion's surface, and Seraphine could see the flicker of something almost reverent in his eyes, before it was quickly masked by his usual cold detachment. "These markings are significant. Sacred geometry uses universal patterns that create everything in our reality."

He let go of the medallion, its weight returning to her chest as he stepped away and went back inside.

Seraphine stood there for a moment, her fingers still gently caressing the edges of the medallion, her eyes lost in the intricate patterns etched into the metal. "What do they mean, I wonder?"

"Ask Evelyn Young."

Seraphine came inside, her hand still resting on the medallion. "Who?"

He didn't look at her as he poured a drink. "Evelyn Young. She's an expert in sacred geometry. I heard she's visiting the planet Forever."

Seraphine's voice dropped to a whisper. "Galen was from Forever. It's a world in the Zavijava star system."

William paused, his expression carefully guarded. After a moment, he seemed to make up his mind. "Evelyn is the proconsul of Beta Canum Venaticorum. She rules over the planet Chara, and all of the other planets in that province. "

Overwhelmed, Seraphine sank into a leather chair. "How could I ever meet the ruler of a province?"

William grinned. "You're forgetting that I'm a Praefect. I shall introduce you."

She looked up at him, her smile returning. "For a price."

"Of course, and a share of profits."

Seraphine looked outside, her gaze fixed on the moon over

Eleutheria. The light cast an ethereal glow over the city. She felt the weight of the medallion once again, its history lingering in her mind like an unanswered question. "How is it that a primitive alien has in her possession a medallion from the lost world of Archon?"

William's mood darkened. "That's a serious question to ask. The Codex of Archon talks about their civilization destroying entire worlds and laying waste to entire regions of the galaxy."

*   *   *

3232 A.D. — YEAR OF THE WATER RAT
(TWO YEARS AGO)
AZURE DRAGON OF THE EAST
HD 154088 / IOUNN

Wearing a white uniform, Captain Seraphine DeVere, the Watcher of the *Brandywine*, looked up into the blue skies and spotted the launch as it came down to land. After saying farewell to a group of the native Iounnians, she reluctantly led her team of contact scientists back to the launch. They had been living in a fairy tale. Now it was time to come out of the dream.

The airlock hissed open and they went inside.

Lieutenant Dominic Fontaine stood at the head of a line of soldiers in the passageway. His face had a strained, painful expression, but Seraphine was too preoccupied to give it much thought. Wishing that she could go back to the dreamland, she mentally shook herself and returned their salutes.

Lieutenant Fontaine asked, "Did you locate the source of the beautiful music we heard when we arrived in this star system?"

Seraphine nodded. "Yes, indeed. It came from the natives of the planet. Iounnians believe that song-lines exist deep within their world, connected to spirit lines that reach into the soul of the planet. They feel a note and sing it into the world. Through song, they channel the energy of the universe into the land, calling forth a dreaming that shapes the reality they all share. I don't know how it travels through space, though. A puzzle for the scientists."

Nkuli Lubanzi, one of the contact scientists, asked, "What do you think that Iounnian meant when he said that all of the song-lines were over?"

Seraphine shook her head. "I have no idea."

Lieutenant Fontaine locked eyes with her, where fantasy collided with reality. "Have you finished the evaluation of the planet, captain?"

Seraphine sighed, feeling as though they had just returned from a peaceful vacation, and struggled to regain her bearings. She nodded. "Yes, Lieutenant. I'll send it in this evening. Thank you for the escort. Now take us back to the *Brandywine*."

* * *

Later, in the quiet solitude of her cabin, Seraphine sat before her computer terminal, an illuminated pane of glass. The only sound was the faint hum of the Brandywine in the background. Lost in thought, she pondered the screen, which read:

WATCHER REPORT

Star System: HD 154088

Planet Name: Iounn

ALIEN SPECIES EVALUATION

Physical: Identical to humans

Intelligence: Equivalent to humans

ESPer Ability: Superior to humans

DANGER EVALUATION

Technology: Primitive

Military Capability: Primitive

Hostility Level: Peaceful

POLICY RECOMMENDATION

Surveillance, Avoidance, Containment or Extermination?

Seraphine leaned back in her chair, gazing out the window of her cabin at the beautiful blue planet, Iounn.

* * *

3234 A.D. — YEAR OF THE WOOD TIGER

(PRESENT DAY)

BLACK TORTOISE OF THE NORTH

GLIESE 783 AB / ELEUTHERIA

Drums beat out a rhythm to techno dance music. Strobe lights flashed, revealing a nightclub full of people partying. Captain Alice White twirled through the crowd, her red hair a fiery blur, caught in a storm of her own making. Her eyes were wide, gleaming with that strange, far-off look, as though she were in the middle of some great, endless story that only she could hear. Clad in a loose, flowing dress that twirled with every step, she spun toward the exit without a care. She was a girl lost in a dream, caught in a world where the stars were just lights in the sky, and the strange, colorful people around her were nothing more than companions on an adventure. Everything was soft and bright, and for Alice, the universe was a treasure chest full of glittering moments, and she was the only one who knew how to open it.

Connected to the nightclub through an adjoining doorway, the Ocean Palace Tavern was full of roguish patrons. Large windows opened the bar up to a view of the ocean, which was bathed in moonlight. Candles cast a warm glow. Dogs drank from stocks of ale with just as much alacrity as the drunks that frequented the tavern. Music from the adjoining nightclub drifted into the tavern. Shtol and Ingli sat at a table. Alice danced in. She skipped over to the bartender and sang a nursery rhyme:

"Three blind mice. Three blind mice.

"See how they run. See how they run.

121

"They all ran after the farmer's wife,

"Who cut off their tails with a carving knife.

"Did you ever see such a sight in your life,

"As three blind mice?"

The bartender, Marcus Boggs, chuckled. "What do you want, Alice?"

Alice glanced at Ingli, who looked as though she had just emerged from the sea. Her damp, tangled blonde hair framed her face like a soft halo, still heavy with the moisture of the ocean. Her dress, once light and airy, now clung to her, the wet fabric accentuating her delicate frame. A towel was draped around her shoulders. She sat quietly, her gaze distant, as though part of her was still somewhere out there, among the waves. Alice dropped her voice down to a conspiratorial whisper, " Someone's having dinner with my first officer."

Marcus glanced at Shtol and Ingli. "So?"

Alice leaned in, her voice soft and vulnerable, like a lost child. "Tell me, Marcus. Do you think she's prettier than I?"

Marcus laughed and poured Alice a mug of rum. "You crazy witch. That girl is an alien."

"Are you sure?"

"That's what Shtol says."

Alice kissed him on the cheek. "Mirror, mirror and all that."

Alice sauntered over to the table where Shtol and Ingli were seated. Alice sat down and pulled out a laser pistol, pointing it at Ingli.

Shtol finally noticed Alice. "Captain White!"

"I'm sorry, am I interrupting?" Alice waved the pistol in a little circle, but it remained pointed at Ingli.

"You need to listen to this, captain."

Alice put on a pouty expression. "Don't you love me anymore, Shtol?"

"DeVere captured an entire load of sunstones in a raid off Bijon Bleu," he announced. "Enough to cripple an entire legion of starships!"

"Messing about with toy soldiers again, Shtol?" Alice adopted a childish tone. "No fair. I want to play!"

Shtol crossed his arms. "Captain, this is serious. The Imperium will hunt us all down if DeVere continues these raids. We need to—"

"I never get in the way of a woman and her prize," said Alice.

Ingli got up. "I'm sorry. I—"

Alice brandished her pistol. "Stay."

Ingli sat back down.

Alice smiled at Ingli. "What world are you from, my pretty?"

"Iouuuu."

"Never heard of it. Is it an external world?"

Ingli was silent.

Alice tilted her head and examined Ingli closely. "If you're truly an inferior, you're the first alien I've met that looks exactly like a human. Where are the rest of your people?"

"They're all dead."

Alice was silent for a moment. She whispered, "I'm sorry."

Ingli looked into Alice's eyes. "You should be."

A long silence stood between them.

"I like her." Alice put away her laser pistol and got up. "Bring her along, Shtol."

All three left the tavern together.

*　　*　　*

Night darkened the turquoise waters of Eleutheria. The moon had set below the horizon. Starships floated in the water of the bay. Alice, Ingli and Shtol approached the schooner and boarded it.

Alice stepped onto the quarterdeck, followed by Shtol, who took a seat at the helm position. Except for the boy, Viktor, who sat at a console, the starship was crewed entirely by aliens. Starsinger Nix, a Ta'Lian, was a tall fairy-like woman sitting at the navigation station. Caesar, a Simsk, cat-like alien, sat at the weapons console. All of the aliens wore translator earrings. New Kingston could be seen through the transparent force field over the star deck.

Alice sat down in the command chair and crossed her legs. She looked up at Ingli. "This is my starship, The Queen of Diamonds," she said. Alice looked at her crew. "Everyone, we have a new friend. Her name's Inglina Nivienne."

The cat-like alien hissed. "Captain White, according to our agreement, you're the only human allowed on this starship."

Alice looked at the boy. "Viktor is human."

Caesar laughed. "Viktor is a slave!"

Alice swiveled her chair to face the boy. "Viktor, why are you on my crew?"

The boy spoke, "I want to explore the stars!"

Her voice dropped to a whisper, "Your dream is your innocence." Alice turned back to face Caesar. "See? He's not a slave. Not really."

Caesar pressed a button on a small hand device and the collar around Viktor's neck glowed. Viktor screamed and fell down to the deck, writhing in pain. All of the alien crew laughed at him. Alice remained silent, not defending the boy. Caesar released the button of his device and Viktor stopped moving. Whimpers of pain came from him.

Nix said, " We tolerate Viktor, but not any other human."

Alice glared at her crew. "Ingli is not human."

"She looks human," said Caesar.

Alice stood up and approached Caesar. She placed her hand on his furry head and she let the caress slide down to his neck. "I'll tell you what she is and I'll tell you what she isn't and you will obey."

Caesar and the others remained silent.

Ingli's gaze fell on Viktor and moved back over to Alice. She whispered, "How can you let them abuse him so?

Alice stepped away from Caesar and sat back down in her chair. Her voice was dreamy and child-like, light and airy, like a dandelion floating through the air. "It will only make him strong."

* * *

Some time later, Ingli walked silently down a passageway and heard weeping. Moving quietly to see, she found Viktor in a small chamber, asleep on the floor. Ingli laid down next to Viktor and put her arms around him. He started awake. She shushed him. He closed his eyes again and they both went to sleep.

* * *

Dawn warmed the turquoise waters of New Kingston harbor. One of the two stars had risen over the horizon. Alice watched the sunrise over Eleutheria. Suddenly, a starship, the *Lethe* took off, bathing the quarterdeck in the glow of its departing anti-gravity engines.

Nix's voice came over the intercom. "Captain, the *Lethe* is departing Eleutheria."

126

Alice sat up. "Let's see where Captain DeVere is going."

The *Lethe* flew up into the morning sky to become one of the stars.

Down in the harbor there was a flash of light and seawater as *The Queen of Diamonds* rose up into the sky in pursuit.

*   *   *

CHAPTER SEVEN
Knight of the Republic

AZURE DRAGON OF THE EAST

HD 172051 / BIJON BLEU

The *Persephone* hung like a delicate pearl in the velvet sea of space. As it orbited the planet Bijon Bleu, the starship gazed down upon a world swathed in green forests and gleaming cities. Starships moved up and down in a constant dance, some dropping down to the the planet's surface, while others rose from the sky palace near the imperial capital. A squadron of sloop 'o war starships soared into space, joining the *Persephone* and the rest of the 9th Legion, a force of ten thousand starships.

A massive instrumentation panel, bristling with scientific readouts, encircled Dominic's office at the aft of the *Persephone*. In the center of the room, a holographic map of the Imperium hovered, displaying over five thousand stars in a network of cold, calculated light. Dominic sat in a chair, gazing up at the star map.

A chime sounded. He waved his hand and a holographic image of the communications officer appeared. "Procuratoris Centenarii Prem Malakar has arrived with the rest of the starships of the 9th Legion. He sends his compliments, sir."

"Give Malakar my best and inform him that I shall meet with him presently," said Dominic.

He closed the communication and returned his gaze to the stars overhead. "Computer, project an observational age metallicity diagram on the star map."

The computer's voice was smooth. "Certainly, master."

The holographic image changed. Each star now had a prismatic display next to it.

Dominic looked at the stars for a moment before speaking. "Computer, are you able to detect cosmic dust residues on the Lethe's hull from our data scans?"

"Yes, master."

An analysis would require an interdisciplinary study, using physics, fractal mathematics, statistical physics and a dozen other scientific disciplines. "Computer, conduct a metallicity study of the cosmic dust residue on the Lethe's hull and display the results."

"Yes, master."

A holographic image of the *Lethe* was displayed. The image focused in upon the starship's hull and readouts appeared. Dominic's words were a hopeful whisper, "Tell me where it came from."

The computer spoke. "There is a 93% probability that the most recent cosmic dust residue on the corsair, Lethe, came from the star system Gliese 783 AB."

"Eleutheria." Dominic smiled. "Computer, project data readouts for each member of DeVere's crew and display their homeworlds."

"Yes, master."

Life-size holographic images for each member of Seraphine's crew appeared, accompanied by their data. The word, "Deceased" appeared next to several of them. Dominic rose from his seat and walked up to stand in front of the healer. Galen's homeworld was Forever in the star system Zavijava.

"Send out Attempt To Locate alerts to the provincial capitals."

"Certainly, master."

"Also send this data to the Free Imperial Knights under my command."

"I remain your humble and obedient servant, master."

A chime from the computer indicated that it has been done.

Dominic waved a hand and the pirate images faded away. He opened a communications channel to the star deck. Captain Septimus Flavius appeared. "How may I serve, Legatus?

Dominic gave his orders. "Signal the legion to break orbit and move beyond the astrosphere of the star. Once we have passed through the termination shock, set our course for Gliese 783 AB."

"Aye, aye, sir."

Accompanied by the 9th Legion, the *Persephone* broke orbit. Solar sails unfurled, catching the stellar wind as the fleet surged forward into the vast emptiness of the star system. Their course was set for the astropause, and beyond it, to another star.

*   *   *

AZURE DRAGON OF THE EAST
ZAVIJAVA / FOREVER

Stars glittered in the darkness. A mandala of light appeared. The *Lethe* emerged from hyperspace. The hypersails retracted, and a melody tuned the solar sails to Zavijva. For a time, everything was still. The starship lingered at the edge of the star system. The crew extended nine masts and raised the solar sails. The *Lethe* sailed towards the colonial world, Forever.

Thousands of starships surrounded Forever like honeybees. A hot white star sank behind the horizon as the *Lethe* crossed into the planet's night side. The starship flipped over and dropped down into the atmosphere.

* * *

A second starship trailed the *Lethe* to the planet but didn't enter the atmosphere. Its hull, gleaming like polished obsidian in the cold light of the star, cut a sleek silhouette against the void. Tracking the *Lethe's* every move with meticulous precision, *The Queen of Diamonds* maintained a cautious orbit, waiting for the other starship to complete its descent.

Alice sat in the captain's chair, eyes sweeping the star deck with quiet satisfaction. Her crew moved like a well-oiled machine—silent, efficient, entirely alien.

At the wheel behind the binnacle, Shtol guided the starship into orbit, his movements fluid and soundless, like a shadow drifting across water. Iridescent skin shimmered in deep teal and sapphire, catching the light in hypnotic glints. Twin lantern-like eyes scanned the void—unblinking, unfathomable. There was always something unsettling about him, something ancient and vast and cold. *He doesn't mean to stare. He's just thoughtful.* Alice felt at ease around him, the way a swimmer surrenders to a gentle current.

Starsinger Nix, a Ta'Lian, emerged from the cathedral at the fore where she had been tuning the solar sails. There was a grace to her that invited awe—a beauty so refined it was easy to forget how easily those clawed hands could part flesh from bone. *She's just misunderstood*, Alice thought.

Caesar lounged on the poop deck like a coiled shadow. The Simsk's amber eyes flicked across the void with a predator's calm. Alice often caught herself assuring new crew members that he wasn't dangerous. Still, no one had ever found the bodies of those who crossed him.

Alice smirked, a little too quickly. Her crew was unlike any other in the galaxy. *People are too quick to judge because aliens scare them. They're not dangerous. Not really.* Leaning back in her chair, she watched the quiet rhythm of her crew.

A presence gathered behind her, almost imperceptible. It was Ingli, her voice a soft whispering in Alice's ear. "I had a dream about you."

A child-like expression crossed Alice's face. Her eyes glazed over as her lips parted, her voice soft and distant. "Was it a happy dream?"

Ingli's voice was soothing. "People were chasing you through a town, angry with you. They carried cruel weapons in their hands. They chased you to the edge of a cliff. You smiled and then you jumped."

"How far did I fall?"

"You flew!"

"Did I?"

"Yes."

Turning around, Alice looked at the cabin boy. "Did you hear that Viktor? I flew like a little bird."

Viktor, wrapped in chains, looked up at her and grinned.

Alice glanced at Shtol. "Take us down—"

Ingli interrupted, "No need to visit this world. Don't you think it'll be easier to follow them when they return to space?"

For a moment, Alice's expression blanked before she nodded. "Yes, indeed," she said, her voice distant. "Remain in orbit for now, Shtol."

Shtol looked at Ingli with suspicion, but nodded just the same. "Aye, aye, captain."

*　*　*

William guided Seraphine through the Imperial Forum of Forever, a vast, sunlit plaza where time seemed to stretch and bend. The air hummed with the rustling of thousands of provincial citizens—humans. Their footsteps were a soft rhythm beneath the towering arches of ancient stone. Around them, robot slaves glided, their metal limbs whispering like wind through the trees, dutifully carrying bundles and parcels. The Zmeyor, with their jade scales glinting in the light, slid through the crowd, their reptilian eyes flicking like lightning between the stalls. Every now and then, an off-world alien would appear, a strange silhouette drifting among the shoppers, as foreign and fleeting as a dream in the waking world.

It was a hot, steamy day. Seraphine looked out at the jungle surrounding the Imperial Forum. "Why do they call this world, Forever?"

"A year lasts 835 solar days here," he said. "Come on, we're almost there."

William guided them toward the basilica, its towering glass walls gleaming like a giant crystalline monument against the vast sky. Provincial soldiers stood rigid at attention, their expressions unreadable beneath their helmets. Without a word, William presented his credentials, the sleek, electronic pass flickering with authorized symbols. The guards examined it briefly, then stepped aside, allowing them to enter the sacred halls without hesitation. The heavy doors slid open, revealing the silent, echoing interior, where secrets waited to be uncovered.

Proconsul Evelyn Young was a youthful woman standing with her back to the door. There was a quiet grace about her, as if she were an essential part of the scene, yet apart from it, waiting for something that only she knew would come. A Vajra Thunderbolt baton of imperial authority rested upon her desk.

Outside, the city was surrounded by sweltering jungles. The air shimmered with the heat, and in its depths, enormous reptilian birds circled lazily, their leathery wings casting fleeting shadows on the ground below. Hovercars zipped past, their engines humming like the distant growl of a great beast. Above, two moons hung low in the sky, pale and solemn, watching over a world teeming with life.

They were ushered in by a reptilian native of the planet.

"Thank you, Jool," said Evelyn.

Jool bowed and left without a word.

William spoke first, "Hello, Evelyn."

"Why have you come in person? I should think—"

Evelyn turned around. When she saw Seraphine, she was startled into momentary silence.

Seraphine raised her eyebrows but remained quiet.

Evelyn found her words again, "Who is this?"

Seraphine bowed to Proconsul Evelyn Young. "I am Seraphine DeVere."

William started to introduce Seraphine, "A trader from—"

Evelyn interrupted him, "Tss-tsst."

Evelyn raised her hand in a swift, commanding motion, signaling for them to take their seats. Seraphine and William settled into sleek, leather chairs positioned across from her, while Evelyn sank gracefully onto a plush couch, her presence commanding, yet composed. Without a word, she tapped a control on the side of the table, and a robot slave silently entered the room, its metallic frame gliding effortlessly over the polished floor. Evelyn glanced at it briefly, her voice calm but firm. "Tea," she instructed, and the slave bowed and went out. Evelyn's smile stretched wide, too polished, too fake, like the grin of a predator toying with its prey.

Seraphine watched, her gaze sharp, feeling the calculated tension in the room. It was all too rehearsed, too perfect. *Let's see how far you want to push this*, she thought, leaning back slightly in her chair and crossing her legs. *You might regret it.*

Though it was as smooth as polished steel, the proconsul's voice was laced with unsettling sweetness. 'I've heard so much about you, centurion. Tell me, why did you decide to become a traitor to humanity?'

Seraphine couldn't help herself. She tilted her head slightly, eyes narrowing, letting a mischievous smirk tug at the corner of her mouth. *Traitor? I'm not going to play your games.*

In one fluid motion, Seraphine was on her feet, the laser pistol already in her hand, aimed squarely at Evelyn's chest.

The look on Evelyn's face didn't change. Not even a twitch.

Seraphine glanced at William. "It was a mistake to come here."

Evelyn remained an immovable pillar of calm. The room felt strangely still, as if a storm was coming. "I permitted you to retain your weapons as a courtesy to Praefect Parker. Was I wrong?"

The proconsul's calm was infuriating. Seraphine backed towards the exit, her laser still pointed at Evelyn. *Oh, you're so cool, too cool.*

138

She had an urge to shoot her just for spite, but resisted the impulse. *This woman probably has no sense of humor.*

The robot slave glided in, its silent movements adding to the disquieting calm. It placed a tray on a nearby table before turning and exiting without a single word. *How quaint*, Seraphine thought. The world continued turning, oblivious to the tension crackling in the room.

Evelyn, as if nothing had happened, calmly poured a cup of tea and set the teapot down with meticulous care. She activated a viewer, and a hologram of Seraphine's face flickered to life in the air between them. Evelyn picked up a cup of tea, took a slow, deliberate sip, and met Seraphine's eyes. "There's an imperial warrant out for your arrest. I have orders to detain you."

Seraphine's smile grew wider. *Oh, she's good.*

William glared at the proconsul. "Stop it, Evelyn!"

Evelyn leaned back in her chair, amused.

Seraphine's mind raced as the pieces clicked into place. Evelyn, with her polished demeanor and commanding presence, was more than just a proconsul—she was William's connection to the underworld. The realization struck her with a quiet intensity. As a proconsul, she was already one of the most powerful people in the Imperium. Seraphine wondered why she had chosen to live as a shadow serving the underworld. Despite her higher rank, Evelyn was pulling the strings in ways Seraphine hadn't anticipated. She was William's superior, his silent master. She glanced at William, wondering why he had chosen to reveal this. *Is he cutting me into a bigger game?* Her laser pistol wavered a few centimeters. "You're offering me a letter of marque? You want me to become a privateer?"

All smiles, Evelyn set her teacup down and rose smoothly from her seat. "Not at all."

Like a panther, she moved toward Seraphine, her steps deliberate and predatory. She placed a hand on Seraphine's shoulder, her touch cool yet firm. "You continue to steal from the Imperium and we'll sell it all back to them. No real harm done."

You think I'm doing this for money? The offer was infuriating and insulting. Seraphine wanted more than that. Phantoms from the past lingered, uninvited, haunting the edges of her mind. *Ah, the faces, always the faces, staring at me. So innocent, so sweet, just before the fire.* But now? Now they were just whispers, everywhere.

Seraphine shook her head. "No."

Seemingly unaccustomed to rejection, Evelyn's eyes turned cold. Her response was tinged with ire, "No?"

William spoke into the silence. "Seraphine, the medallion."

Seraphine's eyes flicked over to William for a second. "What?"

His shout was a surprise. "Give it to her!"

Holstering her weapon, Seraphine took the medallion from

around her neck and tossed it onto the table.

Evelyn picked it up. "What's this?"

"She took it from an inferior. A primitive," said William.

Seraphine forgotten, Evelyn examined the medallion in quiet fascination. She lifted a hand, brushing the air just above an adjacent console. The analysis system shimmered to life, casting soft blue light across her face. A column of holographic data spiraled upward, revealing the medallion's composition. She studied the readout in silence, eyes narrowing. Spectral data danced across the screen in bands of light, each pulse revealing secrets buried for centuries. "These symbols on the medallion are two dimensional flattened versions of three dimensional space."

The computer finished its analysis and a 3D holographic image of a star system with nineteen planets appeared above their heads. Evelyn flipped the medallion over, revealing more symbols. The holographic display shifted to reveal a planet. The Flower of Life symbol appeared on the surface of the world. Evelyn smiled, "Hello."

Seraphine gazed up at the display. "What is this star system?"

Evelyn's words were filled with wonder, "The location of the lost world of Archon."

* * *

3233 A.D. — YEAR OF THE WATER OX

(ONE YEAR AGO)

YELLOW DRAGON OF THE EARTH

THE FORBIDDEN PALACE — SOL / TERRA

The First Citizen, Consul Leopold Voss, stood behind a podium, giving a speech. Next to him stood Captain Seraphine DeVere in a dress uniform, at attention. Dominic stood at attention on the parade ground, along with the rest of the crew of the *Brandywine*.

"I refuse to accept the end of mankind," he declared. "There's a question as old as the earth itself: If someone is trying to kill you, shouldn't you rise up and kill him first? Why not meet aliens in a friendly, loving way? We tried that once. We were nearly exterminated. So we chose strength and we lived. Humanity fights to survive and to thrive in a hostile universe."

It was a sunny day in June but the weather had turned cold. A chilly breeze washed over the parade grounds, disturbing the trees that lined the roadway. Seraphine resisted an urge to run away. She never thought she would be here.

Leopold went on, "Inferior species are fortunate to be governed by a superior race. However, when a superior race is controlled by an inferior species, it leads to oppression. Inferior races, with all of their defects, will always abuse those of superior ability and intellect."

Although Seraphine agreed with his words, she wondered

where the Iounnians would have fit, in imperial society.

The First Citizen paused and looked directly at Seraphine. "The centurions are the finest that humanity has to offer. They are proof of our enduring superiority over alien species. If legend is to be woven around anyone, it should be woven around this centurion who, during a deep exploration mission, has added yet another page to our immortal glorious record."

A golden robot slave stepped forward with a silver box resting on a pillow. Opening the velvet-lined box, Leopold took out a medal. "Captain Seraphine DeVere, you are hereby awarded the Imperial Starburst, our highest medal, for your heroic defense of humanity."

The award would lead to a promotion, too. Seraphine was about to begin training for the Praetorian Guard, the highest military unit in the Imperium. The elite unit was in charge of protecting the two Consuls and they guarded the imperial palace.

Leopold stepped up to Seraphine and pinned the medal on her chest. "Mankind has grown strong in eternal struggle. Only in eternal peace does it perish. The Imperium will either be a galactic power or it will not be at all."

Leopold stepped back, shook her hand and returned her salute. Out of the corner of her eyes, she noticed that Dominic stood at attention, but his face is full of fury.

3234 A.D. — YEAR OF THE WOOD TIGER
(PRESENT DAY)
AZURE DRAGON OF THE EAST
HD 172051 / BIJON BLEU

The *Persephone* led the squadron of sloop 'o war starships. They had recently passed through the termination shock and were inside the hydrogen wall. They approached the astropause, the final boundary between the astrosphere and interstellar space, which was filled with material, especially plasma, not from the local star, but from other stars. They would soon deploy their hypersails and enter hyperspace wormholes on their journey towards the star Zavijava.

Dominic sat in his office, thinking. "Computer, display the alien Ingli Nivienne from star system HD 154088. She is from the fourth planet, Iounn."

"Your wish is my command, master."

The girl's image appeared. *She is quite beautiful.* Dominic had to force himself to think. He walked around the life-size hologram, pondering. Coming around to the front, he stopped to look at her necklace. "Why haven't I noticed this before?"

The computer was silent.

"Tell me about this object."

The computer spoke. "The medallion is made from a rare metallic compound, found only on artifacts from Archon."

Dominic was alarmed. "This medallion came from Archon?"

"Yes, master. Furthermore, the two dimensional symbols inscribed upon it can be extrapolated into three dimensions."

He moved over to a chair and sat down. "What does it reveal?"

"It is the location of an external star system. Phi 1 Pavonis."

"Are there markings on the other side?

"Unknown. I am a pitiable servant, master."

Dominic activated the starship's intercom. Captain Flavius appeared in a holographic window. "Yes, Legatus?"

Dominic thought for a moment, trying to remember the name of the captain of the Shivaji, the flagship of the Ninth Legion. "Send an order to Procuratores Centenarii Prem Malakar," he said. "Have the Ninth Legion follow us to Phi 1 Pavonis. It's an F1 star in the constellation of Pavo."

Captain Flavius frowned. "Sir, that is an external star, far outside the Imperium. It's nearly sixty-nine light years away. At our best speed, it will take us twenty-three solar days to get there."

Once a starship had entered a hyperspace wormhole, it was not possible to change course. Dominic was glad he'd discovered the location of Archon while they were still inside the astrosphere around Bijon Bleu. "That's right Captain. Take us there now."

"Ayc, ayc, sir."

145

AZURE DRAGON OF THE EAST

ZAVIJAVA / FOREVER

William and Seraphine walked next to the glass wall of a sky-scraper by the city's edge. Bird cries came out of the jungle and Seraphine wondered if they were like the prehistoric creatures from earth. As they walked by a bar, she noticed several hover bikes parked in front.

William glanced at her. "What is it?"

Seraphine dropped her playful attitude, momentarily slipping back into her old self. "Mankind has been searching for the lost civilization of Archon for over a thousand years. Perhaps the secrets of the ancients should remain hidden."

William smiled. "Do not fear what you will become. Embrace your destiny."

After she had turned into a pirate, she had found solace in her old instructor, drawn to him because he had fallen into a dark place too. The war had changed him. His remark surprised her. For a brief moment, she saw him as he once was: disciplined, infinitely wise, a force whose every word resonated with quiet authority.

A part of her, still haunted by her past, couldn't help but wonder about his own. "Where were you during the Hymenopteran War?"

He looked into the jungle. "I was on Terra Nova. One night, the bugs came and they bombed Midas City, my home. The flames coming from their bombs spread out like a magic carpet. People were on fire. I couldn't tell if they were men or women."

William noticed a reflection in the glass of the skyscraper. A man with a blaster rifle raised it and took aim at Seraphine. "Imperial assassins!" William pushed her onto the ground.

Energized atomic particles from the blaster rifle struck the side of the building, causing the glass to explode. Tinkling shards of glass flew everywhere, cutting Seraphine. William was cut up badly by the shards of broken glass. Nevertheless, he got up in defiance. A dozen assassins appeared, brandishing an assortment of hand weapons.

William shouted, "Get out of here!"

"What about you?"

"They're here for you. Go!"

William drew his Vajra Thunderbolt baton and transformed it into a sword. He moved with lethal grace, cutting down one attacker after another. Seraphine's heart pounded as she ducked and rolled, narrowly avoiding an energy bolt that struck a fountain nearby, sending a spray of water into the air. There was no time to think—she had to move.

Without hesitation, she leaped onto one of the hover bikes. The engine roared to life beneath her, and she gunned it, the bike surging forward, carrying her away from the chaos. Her breath came faster, her pulse racing with the thrum of the machine. She glanced over her shoulder and saw William retreating, but still holding his ground.

The distant thrum of danger in the air only heightened the urgency. Then, a flicker of movement in the rearview mirror caught her attention—an assassin stepped into the open, his rifle aimed straight at her. A cold chill ran down her spine. She could see it in the reflection—he was calm, unfazed, as if this was all part of some cold, inevitable calculation.

Energy bolts streaked out. Seraphine swerved hard, adrenaline surging as she pushed the hover bike's throttle to its limit. The deadly bolt whizzed by, missing her. The wind howled in her ears, but she forced herself to focus. *Just make it to the jungle. Just a little further.*

The edge of the jungle was close now. The treeline loomed ahead, a sliver of safety. She could almost taste it, the warm relief of cover, the whisper of the trees, the birds crying out.

Without warning, an energy bolt struck home. The hover bike shuddered violently and there was a blinding flash of light. An explosion erupted with a deafening roar, hurling Seraphine into the air.

* * *

Gisele lay in bed, wrapped in Sebastian's arms. As thy kissed, the intercom chimed. She ignored it. The chime sounded again and she broke off the kiss.

Gisele woke up in her cabin with a start, realizing that she had been having a dream. She was drained of energy and disoriented. She looked around for Sebastian but realized that she was alone. The intercom chimed again. She rolled out of bed and hit the intercom. "What is it?"

Christian's voice was full of concern. "Trouble."

* * *

The white star Zavijava had sunk beneath the horizon, casting the jungle into a dense twilight, where shadows stretched like dark, creeping tendrils. Seraphine's muscles ached as she crawled through the undergrowth, her body low to the ground, each movement measured and silent. Her hand instinctively reached for her side, only to find the reassuring weight of her laser pistol missing. *Well, that's just perfect*, she thought.

The sound of footsteps reached her ears, deliberate and heavy, cutting through the rustling quiet of the jungle. Her grin grew as she rolled onto her back. "If you're trying to scare me, it's not working."

The imperial assassin loomed above her like some dark sentinel from a nightmare. His rifle lowered slowly, the barrel pointed straight at her chest with the kind of precision only a trained killer

149

could manage.

Seraphine tilted her head, feigning curiosity. "So," she teased, "is this the part where you shoot me or do we dance a little first?"

The assassin's expression was cold, impassive.

But Seraphine didn't flinch. She never did.

* * *

In the hold of the *Lethe*, some of the crew had gathered. Gisele walked in and saw Sebastian. She walked by him without saying anything to him. Christian was pulling the covers off three hover-bikes. Sebastian asked, "Where are the rest of the crew?"

Gisele answered him. "They're out in the city."

Christian said, "Someone took a shot at the captain."

Crossing her arms, Gisele raised her eyebrows. "How would you know?"

"I had an observation drone follow her."

Sebastian retrieved a blaster pistol and laser rifle from a weapons rack. He tossed a blaster pistol to her and she caught it. Sebastian went over to a hoverbike and got on.

Christian opened the cargo hatch to a world in twilight. One moon could be seen rising over the horizon.

Gisele glared at him. "Stalking the captain? We'll have to have a chat about that."

He got onto the hoverbike next to Sebastian. "That'll be fun."

150

Gisele glared at him as he zoomed out of the cargo bay.

Sebastian looked over at her from his hoverbike. "You coming?"

*   *   *

The assassin stood with his rifle pointed down at Seraphine. A searing flash of light erupted, and in an instant, he was gone. Seraphine blinked, the bright afterglow lingering in her vision before the darkness swallowed her once more.

Footsteps approached, deliberate and unhurried. Seraphine looked up, her grin flashing in the dim light, and there stood Celestine Ney, disintegrator rifle still smoking in her hands. A tiny black drone appeared, following Celestine like a puppy. It focused its camera on Seraphine, recording everything.

"Thanks," said Seraphine.

Celestine threw down a pair of handcuffs. "You're welcome."

*   *   *

Covered in moonlight, dozens of starships sat on the landing field of the sky palace. Her hands bound, Seraphine walked towards Celestine's starship, the *Patriote*. It was a sleek corsair. Celestine was behind, motivating Seraphine to move forward. The tiny drone followed them quietly.

As they stepped out onto the landing field, a laser beam struck Celestine's force field. Celestine jumped out of the way. Seraphine tried to run, but Celestine drew a laser pistol, set it to stun and shot her in the back. Seraphine fell down.

There was a whirring of approaching hoverbikes. Christian and Gisele zoomed by. Celestine shot a spherical bolt of plasma into their path. Gisele avoided it but Christian did not. He struck the plasma field head on. His hoverbike exploded and he was thrown to the ground.

Gisele spun around to aim her laser rifle. Celestine changed her energy shield into a reflective mirror. Gisele shot and the laser bolts bounced off the shield. Gisele jumped off her hoverbike and hit the ground hard. One of the reflected laser bolts struck the hover bike, cutting it in half.

Celestine activated a Heads Up Display on her helmet, and searched for her adversaries. Three blips were nearby. One was directly behind her.

Sebastian struck Celestine with a molecular edged sword, but her shield protected her. Celestine twirled around. She drew her thunderbolt and it transformed into an ice spear, just as her shield collapsed. His sword struck the spear and she held it there for an instant. She looked into his eyes and said, "Not satisfied with my offer?"

"No."

The ground turned slippery with ice. Sebastian fell onto his back. Celestine pointed her spear at his chest. "What do you want?"

Sebastian glared at her. "More!"

He knocked the spear away, rolled over and jumped to his feet. Celestine struck the ground and everything for a hundred meters turned to ice. Sebastian had trouble staying on his feet. At that moment, Celestine lunged at him with the spear. Rather than parrying it, he fell onto his back again and rolled out of the way. Celestine struck him in the side of the head with her spear and he fell down, stunned.

Celestine pressed a button on her battle armor, activating an anti-gravity belt and flew up into the air. She spied Seraphine on the ground, unconscious and landed next to her. Kneeling down, she retracted the thunderbolt into a baton, and placed her antigravity belt on Seraphine.   Celestine walked back to her starship with Seraphine floating behind her. A light on her Heads Up Display came on just as Sebastian stepped out from behind the *Patriote*. He took aim with a blaster rifle and fired.

*   *   *

Seraphine opened her eyes and sat up. Celestine lay nearby on the ground.

Christian and Sebastian approached. Christian helped Seraphine get to her feet while Sebastian looked down at Celestine's body. A smoking hole in her chest revealed a machine underneath. "She's an android," whispered Sebastian.

153

"Plague and perish her," grumbled Christian. "I've heard of some bounty hunters using android bodies. They can transfer their consciousness into them at the speed of light. If the android is destroyed, they simply wake up."

Sebastian looked into the sky. "I wonder where she is?"

Seraphine watched the tiny drone observing them from above the landing field. For a moment, it remained there, as if to verify that Celestine had failed to catch her prize. Then it whizzed off, towards the city. Seraphine sighed. "Great, an audience. Nothing like a little pressure to spice things up."

With a loud sigh, Christian holstered his weapon. "Have you ever considered the advantages of being somewhere else, captain?"

Seraphine smiled. "Time to leave this world."

*   *   *

CHAPTER EIGHT
Archon

SOUTHERN ASTERISMS — PHI 1 PAVONIS / ARCHON

The *Persephone* led the legion of ten thousand starships, cutting through the hydrogen wall surrounding the star system. Nineteen planets danced in orbit around the white star, Phi 1 Pavonis. Inside the starships' vast, dark cathedrals, the starsingers' melodies rang out, resonating through great chambers as they tuned the sails to match the exact frequency of the star. This allowed the fleet to achieve optimal speed within the star system. The hypersails were retracted, and once the solar sails were tuned, the starships extended them into space to catch the light of the star. The fleet sailed onward towards the inner planets.

Dominic could feel the tension in the air as the sound of marching boots echoed in the corridors of the *Persephone*. As he and Inanna came out onto the star deck, the view beyond the transparent force field took his breath away. In a whisper of awe, he murmured, "Archon."

The planet exuded a quiet, haunting beauty. Archon was a jewel drifting in the void, its surface a striking mix of vibrant green and soft, earthy tones. Vast continents, now silent and still, hinted at a time when they shimmered with the richness of life, framed by winding rivers and great, tranquil seas. The pyramids and towers of the ancient cities stood in silent testament, surrounded by nature that had long since reclaimed the land. The ancient rulers had vanished, leaving only the whispers of their legacy in the shadows.

A lieutenant looked up from his display. "Our probes report this world is devoid of sentient life, but it's covered with ancient cities."

Captain Flavius Septimus turned to look at Dominic. "It looks like you were right, sir."

Inanna raised an eyebrow. "When is he not? Behold! The planet Archon."

Dominic looked at her, noticing a strange expression—pride mingled with defiance, burning in her heart like a smoldering fire. She wore the moment like a crown. What was she seeing that he couldn't?

Captain Flavius brought Dominic's attention back. "We may have found Archon, but how will we know where they'll land?"

"Our information is incomplete," said Dominic. "We shall wait. Send an order to Procuratores Centenarii Malakar. Have the 9th Legion place gravity mines at strategic locations. Report any disruptions in the astrospheric current sheet from arriving vessels. Keep our starships out of sight until I call for them."

"Aye, aye, sir."

Dominic glanced at the holographic display of the star system, which hovered over the binnacle. He gave an order to the helm officer. "Move the Persephone behind the largest moon of Archon, Lieutenant."

"Aye, aye, sir."

* * *

The *Lethe* emerged from the hyperspace vortex at the edge of the star system. The sleek corsair, painted black to blend in with the void, flickered momentarily in the cold emptiness before retracting its hyper sails. The ship's solar sails unfurled, catching the distant light of Phi 1 Pavonis as it propelled itself toward Archon, a mere pinprick against the backdrop of space. Beneath the watchful eyes of the starships guarding the planet, the *Lethe* slipped through the picket line like a shadow—silent, unnoticed.

*   *   *

A stone monument within a sea of glass, a massive pyramid dominated a city where dozens of tall glass buildings stretched out in every direction. Seraphine and some of her crew walked through the streets of the deserted city. Gisele paused to look up at the abandoned buildings. "So, this is Archon."

"Yes," said Seraphine. She looked at a bird of prey high up in the sky, circling. "This city was a ghost town a thousand years before we ever traveled to the stars."

They passed by a park that contained a playground. Sebastian stopped to look at it. He picked up an abandoned toy from where grass had grown around it. "This park, now so peaceful, must have rung with life and the laughter of children."

"The Archons are all dead now," said Gisele. "Extinct."

Sebastian looked up at the sea of glass and stone. "Even so, I can imagine it ringing still."

They come to a citadel . It was a beautiful building made out of marble and glass. The building had a large Flower of Life symbol carved into stone over the entryway. Seraphine picked up the medallion from around her neck and examined it. The symbols were the same. "We're here. This is the place indicated on the medallion."

They entered a wide foyer dominated by a towering wall panel. At its base were several disk-shaped depressions, their purpose unclear. Gisele stepped forward and traced her finger through the dust that coated the panel's surface. "What do you suppose happened to the Archons?"

Sebastian glanced around the room. "Who can say?"

Seraphine stood transfixed before the ancient panel, a nameless unease stirring deep within the shadowed recesses of her mind. A creeping sense of dread came upon her, primitive and insistent. The medallion at her throat, which she had once regarded as a mere relic, now pulsed with a terrible power, far darker than anything she had anticipated. She grasped it, feeling the cold metal seep into her skin. *This is no simple trinket*, she thought. *It's a key to something vast and incomprehensible—something waiting, perhaps, for me to open it.* For a moment, she considered walking away. Just as quickly, she abandoned the thought. Slowly, she removed the medallion from around her neck and placed it into one of the depressions.

It fit perfectly.

The console lit up, revealing the hieroglyphic writing of the Archons. A section of the wall beside the console slid open, revealing a transportation tube. Without hesitation Seraphine stepped forward.

Christian, who had been silent for most of the day, finally spoke. "You want to get in there?"

Seraphine's lips twitched into a thin smile, her eyes remained locked on the tube. She paused for a heartbeat, savoring the moment, before tilting her head slightly. "Yeah, why not?"

"You're crazy! You think it's still working?" said Christian. "How old is this place?"

Gisele chuckled. "Come on."

They got inside and the door slid shut.

* * *

The walls were worn with time, the brass fixtures glinted faintly in the low, ambient light as Dominic walked down a passageway on the *Persephone*. Emerging onto the star deck, he glanced through the transparent force-field at the solar sails. Whispering in the vacuum, they lingered in moon shadow.

Suddenly, his communicator chimed. He turned aft towards his cabin as he replied, "Fontaine here."

The urgent voice of Captain Flavius came over the intercom. "We have detected movement on the surface of Archon. I can't understand how they could've slipped through our blockade. It could be an error, sir, but I wanted to inform you."

Dominic smiled with a touch of admiration. "No, Captain, its not a mistake," he said. "Call the fleet out from hiding."

"Aye, aye, sir."

* * *

Seraphine and the others stepped into an immense chamber, its vastness swallowed by the oppressive darkness. The walls, lined with shelves, bore countless spherical crystals, all black. Their smooth surfaces seemed to absorb the dim light. Upon a central dais sat a single, smaller crystal sphere, its surface etched with the intricate Flower of Life symbol. A faint, eerie glow kindled within it as Seraphine picked it up.

Sebastian's voice strained with tension. "What is it?"

It was unnaturally cool. A sudden chill crept up her arm as she held it up to the light. "It's a data crystal, but it has a coded lock. I can't open it."

Christian looked at it closely. "What do you think it contains?"

Seraphine's breath caught, and for a fleeting moment, the realization of what she held in her hand weighed down upon her. She shrugged it away. "Plans for the construction of Archon bombs, most likely," she muttered, "or something equally horrible."

Christian's grin spread wide, an excited glint in his eyes. "We're rich! Many's the long night I've dreamed of—"

Seraphine's voice cut through the air, interrupting him. "What blood and sorrow and lies and shame and cruelty will spring from this little crystal sphere? No, we can't let the Imperium have this."

"Why not? They already have Archon bombs," said Christian.

Seraphine shook her head. "The treasure hunter Captain Black discovered an ancient warship, but he recovered only a few of the Archon bombs. The Imperium hasn't been able to duplicate the weapons. They will eventually run out. So no, we can't let them have this."

"Then, by thunder, why are we here?"

"To destroy this crystal."

Christian's hand hovered near his blaster, a flash of recklessness in his eyes. Without warning, he drew it, pointing it at Seraphine.

Gisele drew her laser pistol, aiming it squarely at Christian. "Think carefully."

Seraphine met Christian's eyes with an unsettling calm. "Have you ever seen the detonation of an Archon bomb?"

"No."

A dark memory surfaced in Seraphine's mind. She closed her eyes, momentarily lost in the nightmare that haunted her. She whispered, her voice a fragile thing, as if speaking it aloud might summon the horror anew. "The way they work is they start a chain fission reaction in a specific element such as uranium or carbon or even hydrogen. It takes several solar days to engulf a planet in the nuclear firestorm." Her voice trailed off and she opened her eyes, the unimaginable fires still flickering behind them.

They stood there in the dark chamber, weapons drawn. Christian's blaster trembled slightly in his grip, but Gisele's aim was unflinching. Neither dared to move.

The weight of the crystal was heavy in Seraphine's palm.

162

Then came a sound—soft, deliberate, almost imperceptible. Somewhere close.

Too close.

Alice White and her crew emerged from the transport shaft, weapons leveled at Seraphine's crew, who were caught off guard.

All except for Sebastian. He was gone. Seraphine hadn't seen him move, but he was no longer where he'd been a moment ago.

"You forgot to invite me to your party," said Alice, her voice sweet but laced with a strange, unsettling edge. "But I'm not angry at you. Not really." Her demeanor was almost childlike, but her eyes were cold. "Can we play? Give us your toys."

Seraphine and her crew slowly lowered their weapons to the floor.

"Ooh, how pretty." Alice sauntered up to Seraphine and plucked the data crystal out of her hand. A wicked grin spread across Alice's face as she tossed the crystal to Ingli, who caught it with surprising grace. Alice turned to her crew, a gleam in her eye and a wolfish smile curling her lips. "Lay to it boys!"

Viktor stepped forward and tied Seraphine's hands with rough efficiency. Nearby, Nix and Caesar bound Gisele and Christian, while Shtol stood watch with a laser rifle, unmoving.

Seraphine locked eyes with Viktor.

The boy smiled. "Hello, stupid."

Seraphine remembered him. "You're the one with the leash."

Viktor's smile faltered. He fingered the collar at his throat, then yanked her bonds tighter with a flash of anger.

Alice let out a light laugh. "So you've noticed my mascot, have you? We found him in a lifeboat near a destroyed passenger liner." She leaned in, her voice a low murmur of dark amusement. "He brings me luck."

Shtol pointed his laser rifle at Seraphine.

In quiet defiance, she looked away, eyes settling upon Ingli.

The girl cradled the crystal with quiet wonder, as if it were something sacred.

The girl looked up. Their eyes met.

A soft smile, laced with innocence, touched Ingli's lips.

As she tilted the crystal slightly, light caught its surface and brushed against her face like the kiss of an angel.

A chill crept down Seraphine's spine.

What nightmare will she bring?

*   *   *

Inanna stood beside Septimus on the command deck, her expression hard as cut stone. "Captain, deploy Imperial warbots to the surface of Archon."

He hesitated.

"I serve as centurion under Legatus Legionis Fontaine," she

said, her tone cool and precise. "That grants met he rank of Legatus. I've given you an order, Captain."

With a shallow nod, he replied, "Aye, aye."

Moments later, the heavens came alive with light. Hundreds of brief, brilliant flares burst from the undersides of the *Persephone* and the other starships arrayed in orbit. Sleek drop pods streaked into the atmosphere, trailing fire. One by one, the cylinders descended into the silent city below, fanning out through crumbling streets and broken towers like steel locusts set loose upon a forgotten harvest.

*   *   *

Viktor kept to the edge of the corridor, small and silent. The slave collar pressed against his throat, but he didn't touch it, not with the crew watching. He knew the rules. *Don't speak. Don't stare. Don't get in the way.*

Alice walked beside Seraphine as they led the crew through the towering foyer, side by side like old friends at a masquerade. Her voice was light, but there was something sharp beneath it. "So, you were an Imperial Watcher."

Seraphine didn't look at Alice. "Yes, long ago I was the captain of a scout ship, the Brandywine."

Across the foyer, Viktor spotted a shadow moving along the far wall. One of Seraphine's crew, moving like a cat. There was a cold glint of metal.

Sebastian had taken aim.

Alice came to a halt suddenly. The entire group stilled, like puppets on invisible strings. "Judge, jury and executioner."

Seraphine turned fast, her boots scraping the floor. "I was an explorer!"

Alice tilted her head, calm, disbelieving. "How many worlds did you explore into oblivion?"

Sebastian hesitated. His rifle lowered a fraction. He seemed entranced by Alice, unable to shoot. Viktor smirked. *He likes her.*

Light streamed through the glass walls, too bright, too quiet. Beyond the foyer, an Imperial warbot glided into view—silent, calculating, lost in the glare.

No one else seemed to notice. The light was blinding, fractured through glass into a haze that washed over everything. Viktor did. He watched it warily.

Seraphine straightened up. Her voice was colder now, mechanical. "Extermination is authorized only when aliens pose a threat to humanity."

"That's not what I've heard," said Alice. "I heard the Imperium is going around nuking anyone they don't like."

Seraphine's expression tightened, her voice rising. "We have to defend ourselves."

Alice gave a short laugh. "Is that what you call it?"

166

"It's called living or dying," snapped Seraphine. "Do you want to live? Do you want your family to live? Do you want humanity to survive? Because aliens—" She stopped, just for a breath. "—aliens are dangerous."

Outside the warbot halted, hovering in place. The gun turret rotated toward the building.

Still, no one saw.

"Better safe than sorry," said Alice. "You side with the Imperium but you're outraged by them at the same time."

Seraphine looked away.

Alice shook her head. "And people call me crazy."

A moment of silence passed.

Alice's frown deepened, her voice turning quiet. "If you agree with the Imperium so much, why are you waging a private war against them? Why are you a pirate?"

Seraphine shook her head. Her next words came out heavy with sorrow. "We planted paradise among the stars. Now they see only weeds to pull. We were a light in the darkness, but the Imperium lost its way. We went to the stars full of dreams. Now it's all fire and ash."

Viktor saw something flicker in her face. *Rage? Or sadness? Maybe both.*

Alice's voice was quiet, but sharp. "You're angry they became monsters, but you still talk like one."

Seraphine faltered for half a second. Then her voice rose, defensive. "Take your morals and apply it to human beings. Not to inferior alien vermin."

The warbot's turret locked into place.

Viktor waved his arms and shouted. "Hey!"

Everyone ignored him.

The warbot's blaster cannon hummed as it charged.

Viktor froze.

Alice's voice turned soft. "Who did you lose in the war?"

Seraphine shouted, "Everyone!"

The warbot fired.

The sound was deafening. An earsplitting roar, followed by an explosion ripped through the air, overwhelming everything. The entire wall disintegrated in a blinding white-hot glow. The force of the blast sent shockwaves through the building

Viktor was thrown to the ground, his arms instinctively covering his head as the air turned to fire.

Through the smoke, the shape of the warbot emerged, tall, gleaming, precise.

The second beam cut through the air above them. The shot completely disintegrated what remained of the wall, causing some of the building to collapse in a torrent of dust and debris.

Viktor pushed himself up, panic rising in his throat. Without thinking, he leapt over the rubble and sprinted toward the massive breach in the wall. Out of the corner of his eye, he caught the shimmer of movement. The warbot's turret was tracking him. He didn't stop. He didn't look back. He ran into the burning daylight beyond.

*   *   *

Seraphine caught Christian's attention. With her bound hands, she pointed at the hole in the wall where they might make their escape. Christian nodded with understanding. Seraphine ran into the lobby, past the hovering warbot. She slapped it on the side as she went by. "Come get me!"

Seraphine ran outside, followed by a disintegrator beam, which struck the building across the street. A huge section of the wall vanished and the building collapsed. The warbot followed her outside.

Sprinting past empty stores and deserted cafes, Seraphine glanced behind at the hovering warbot as it swiveled its turret to take aim at her back. Stumbling down to strike the white pavement, she rolled out of the way as a blue white flash went by. A small building at the far end of the street vanished in a burst of heat and light, leaving only a cloud of particles drifting through the air.

Seraphine got up and ran down the street, only to find another warbot. She turned down a side street and came to a river. Glancing over her shoulder, she could see a warbot coming into view from around a corner. She took a deep breath and jumped into the river.

The water was cold, and she had trouble holding her breath. Through the ripples above, she saw a warbot reach the river's edge. She dove deeper into the water and let the current carry her away.

Seraphine swam as best she could with her wrists tied together. A predatory fish, similar to a shark, pursued her. She kicked it in the head and it passed by, circling around for another attack. Energy beams from disintegrators crisscrossed underwater. One hit the predator, killing it.

She dove deeper until the world turned green and dim. A drifting field of river weeds offered cover, and she vanished into it like a shadow.

*   *   *

Viktor rose from a pile of rubble, shook off the dust, and got up just as a warbot appeared. "I'm going to die in a courageously awesome way!"

He ran off, climbed a wall and jumped out of the way of a disintegrator beam, which caused a huge explosion. Viktor slipped down a pole, bounced off a low wall and tumbled to the ground. Rising once more, he sprinted across an empty street. Finding a deserted place, he leaned against the wall and tried to remove his collar—to no avail. Seeing a metal bar in a pile of rubble, he picked

170

it up and tried to pry it off, only to drop it at the sight of another warbot.

Viktor ran down a street and saw Caesar running in the opposite direction.

An explosion knocked Caesar to the ground. His blaster landed next to Viktor.

Picking it up, Viktor motioned with the blaster for Caesar to get up and remove his collar.

Caesar let out a low growl. He withdrew the collar control unit and got up. There came a humming sound. As Caesar crept forward, a warbot glided by.

For an instant, Viktor's eyes followed the warbot.

Caesar knocked the blaster out of his hands.

Viktor grabbed the collar control unit out of Caesar's hands and ran away down the street. He heard Caesar chasing after him. Just as he had come to the end of an alley, Viktor felt Caesar's hand on his shoulder.

There came another explosion.

Viktor felt himself tumbling to the ground.

He crawled under a pile of debris to hide.

Amid a flurry of smoke and debris, he saw Caesar run off in another direction.

The warbot whizzed off after him.

Some time after, Viktor crept to the edge of a crater, sat down on a pile of rubble and examined the collar control unit. He pressed a button and the collar fell off. He picked it up and threw it away with a shout of joy.

Alice ran into view and dove past Viktor into the crater. A pursuing warbot appeared. Stopping at the lip of the crater, it swiveled it's turret around and pointed it at Alice, who was too exhausted to run. She lay there, looking up at the machine, waiting for the end to come.

Rather than running away, Viktor picked up a rock and threw it at the warbot . The rock bounced off the metal machine harmlessly.

Distracted, the warbot swiveled its weapon around towards him.

He closed his eyes.

*   *   *

Christian and Gisele entered the *Lethe* through an open door. Outside, distant flashes appeared, accompanied by the sounds of disintegrator beams and crumbling buildings. Christian looked around. "Where's Sebastian?"

Gisele paused to catch her breath. "I saw him running after captain White. There was a strange look in his eyes."

Christian walked over to a weapons locker and picked up a heavy blaster rifle. "Tell the crew to get the starship ready for a quick departure. We may have to burn a sunstone to escape this time. I'm going out to find the captain."

"Aye, aye, sir."

*　*　*

Seraphine leaned into the engine compartment of the bright gold hovercar from the *Lethe*, parked along the empty street. A steady stream of water dripped from her clothes, splashing onto the white pavement beside the vehicle. Soaking wet, she could feel the material of her white cotton blouse cling to her skin. Her leather boots and pants seemed heavier too. A long tangle of wet hair was blocking her view, so she snapped her head around in an attempt to swing it out of the way. She bit her lip, mumbling out a complaint about having to work with her hands tied together. Finally, she stepped back and closed the compartment.

She would have liked to have made some kind of gesture with her arms, but didn't bother. She sat down onto the hard sun baked pavement, wishing that it would warm her up, but a cool breeze that made the trees near the road move slowly back and forth wouldn't permit her any surcease. Shivering, she wanted to cross her arms, but again, couldn't move how she had wanted to. Tilting her head, she wondered if the device would work. Axion Spin Field Generators could be a bit tricky to interfere with. Still, it wasn't really a bomb that she had made. It was more like a—*what? I've never seen a pulse*

173

of distorted spacetime.

The object of her attention was soon seen gliding around the corner of the far intersection, it's bright gray turret swiveling back and forth, searching. Narrowing her eyes, she wondered if it had seen her yet.

Getting slowly to her feet, she carefully moved over to the hovercar, turning on the engine and pointing the car at the distant machine. The warbot was about a hundred yards away, but it had just turned in her direction. "Here goes," she muttered.

The hovercar shot off down the street towards the robot, which studiously ignored it.

Seraphine knotted her eyebrows together, wondering at the machine's inattentiveness but then realized why it had ignored the vehicle.

It missed.

*   *   *

Alice barely registered the clatter of the stone as Viktor hurled it at the machine. The warbot turned—too fast. Its turret rotated toward the boy. He just stood there, defiant, and it brought a smile to her lips.

The explosion ripped through the silence like a drumbeat of doom. Smoke and metal shrieked into the air. Alice flinched, arms raised instinctively as shards whistled past her. She blinked against the haze, ears ringing.

Then—movement.

Out of the smoke stepped a man. He emerged like a ghost from a forgotten war, tall and pale, wreathed in the steam and grit of the ruined street. His coat whipped behind him in the breeze. In his hands, a blaster rifle smoked. The smell of ozone clung to him like a second skin. He climbed down into the crater and reached for her.

Alice didn't resist. She let him lift her, too stunned to speak. His arms were steady, unnervingly warm. He carried her out of the smoke as though she weighed nothing, then set her down gently on the pavement beside Viktor's small, still body.

She gathered the boy close and pressed her cheek to his hair. "Someday," she murmured, half to herself, half to the wind, "I won't love you anymore."

The city groaned around them. Distant buildings collapsing, disintegrator fire screeching in the distance.

She looked up at the stranger.

His face was unreadable, but something was in his eyes—not pity, not anger, but it was something else. *Was it love?*

"Who are you?"

He turned his head, scanning the distance. A warbot was closing in, whirring over the rubble. He raised his rifle again. "I am Sebastian," he said. "Your shipmates went that way."

175

"Why are you helping me?"

"I won't let them hurt you."

The warbot crested the rubble. Before it could fire, Sebastian squeezed the trigger. A bolt of charged particles cut through the air. The machine erupted in a bloom of fire and metal.

Alice didn't wait. Cradling Viktor against her chest, she ran, vanishing into the smoke before she could think better of it.

*   *   *

Sighing loudly, Seraphine glanced down a side street, wondering which way to run. A brief thought of returning to the river was brushed aside just as quickly as it had come. *I nearly drowned last time.*

A distant, "Crump!" sound brought her attention back towards the hovercar, which had just rammed into the far building. The warbot paused a moment, its turret swiveling around to look at the wrecked hovercar.

Then it happened.

It wasn't an explosion really. It was more like a mirror that began to twist out of shape, distorting the view of the neighborhood. It became more intense and then it seemed to snap, causing everything to expand in a surreal wave, rippling out in every direction. The warbot was instantly crushed as if a giant hand had reached down to squash it. All of the buildings on the street block disappeared in a silent white puff of smoke and debris, which projected slices of rubble and metal shrapnel. The low rumbling sound came next, a wave of violent noise rushing past with the wind.

Something struck Seraphine's forehead with a painful jolt, causing her legs to give out. She found herself on her knees, staring at the devastation. Reaching up to rub the pain away, she realized that she couldn't move her arms independently. She dropped them down, staring blankly at her bound hands, which were now covered in blood. Disoriented, she couldn't remember who had tied her hands together, or why she had been bound. *What happened?*

The rumbling sound began to die out, and when she looked up again, the street was empty of any buildings. Everything within a hundred meters of the crash had been pulverized. Seraphine could feel something warm trickling down into her eyes, and attempted to wipe it away, but couldn't keep the blood out of her eyes. She glanced up again at the ruined neighborhood. The exclamation came unbound from her startled lips, "Wow!"

Sinking down to sit on the white pavement, she noticed that there was now a gaping crater in the street. The spacetime disruption had spread off in every direction. She shook her head. "Maybe that wasn't such a good idea."

A powdery residue began to rain down, gently coating her water logged blouse with a fine white blanket. Her breathing became

177

heavy. She tried to will away the darkness clouding her eyes but everything was spinning. Seraphine's lips parted into a smile. Feeling intoxicated, she giggled just a little bit before whispering quietly to herself, "Oops."

At last, the darkness finally came. Seraphine fell down into the street.

* * *

Dominic walked up to a display manned by a lieutenant. An area of desolation appeared in one of the cities and was growing larger.

"What's going on, Lieutenant?"

"A region of distorted space-time has appeared on the planet, sir."

"How?"

"Unknown. The region is expanding. I can't tell how large it will become before it extinguishes itself."

Dominic noticed another display, which showed the progress of the hundreds of warbots on the planet. Captain Flavius walked over. "Our assault is going well, sir."

"What's going on?" he asked. "Who ordered this attack?"

"I did."

Dominic turned around and saw Inanna Silva standing there with a faraway expression in her face. Dominic signaled Captain

Flavius to leave them alone. Septimus stepped away.

As soon as Dominic was alone with Inanna, he grabbed her and shoved her against the wall, holding her there. "What have you done?"

A playful smile lit up Inanna's face, as if it were just a game. "Your past is holding you back. I gave the order because I knew you were unable to."

For an instant, Dominic imagined that he could see a glittering woman standing besides Inanna, whispering in her ear. He shook his head and blinked. The shining one was no longer there. "It was my decision."

"You are a great man. You are the one who has discovered Archon," she said. "Forget the past. Follow me into the future."

Dominic let go and turned away.

Inanna spoke in a reasonable voice. "You can't let the technology of Archon fall into the hands of a pirate, can you?"

Dominic waved to the captain and he came over. "Yes, Legatus?"

"Recall the warbots."

Inanna came over and leaned close to Dominic. "Why not have them sweep the surrounding areas before they return to the fleet?"

Dominic glared at her for a moment. "Follow my orders, Captain."

"Aye, aye, sir."

*   *   *

3232 A.D. — YEAR OF THE WATER RAT (TWO YEARS AGO)
AZURE DRAGON OF THE EAST — HD 154088 / IOUNN

Seraphine sat in the command chair. Through the viewscreen, the planet Iounn could be seen. Officers sat at displays. A flash of light appeared among the stars. The San Isodoro, a ship 'o the line battleship, sailed into view. Seraphine stood up, surprised. "Tell them to stand down, Lieutenant."

The officer glanced over his shoulder at Seraphine. "They say they're under orders, ma'am."

There was a small flash on the side of the battleship.

Seraphine shouted, "No!"

An Archon bomb fell slowly into the planet's atmosphere.

"Gunner, target the device entering the planet's atmosphere."

"I'm sorry, captain. The object is out of range."

*   *   *

Dominic sat alone at a console, eyes fixed on the burning image of the planet suspended in the holographic display. Light from the projection cast faint, shifting patterns across his face. There was a trace of orange fire there, too, growing in size.

The door opened.

Seraphine stormed in, boots striking the floor. Her voice quiv-

180

ered with rage as she stopped in front of him. "What have you done?"

He got up to face her. "I have made a decision that you could not."

"What are you talking about?"

After a brief silence, he said, "I changed your report on this world from 'Surveillance' to 'Exterminate.'"

"Why? They're beautiful. They're all so beautiful."

"Indeed they are attractive," he said. "Hypnotically so. Think about their powers of persuasion, Captain. How they manipulate us so easily. They are a race of hypnotists. If they reach humanity, how long do you think it will be until they're ruling the Imperium? Their beauty shall enslave us all"

Seraphine shoved Dominic against the wall. "You're murdering millions of innocent people."

Dominic chuckled. "I sent up a bottle of champagne. Once you realize I'm right about them, you'll celebrate the destruction of another one of the enemies of mankind."

Seraphine punched him in the face. He slid down to the floor, unconscious. She drew her blaster and pointed it at him. She stood there, trembling, for a moment. Unable to do it, she closed her eyes and holstered it again. Turning around, she went out.

✶   ✶   ✶

Wearing the uniform of an Imperial Scout Captain, Seraphine stepped out onto the star deck, one hand dripping blood. She walked over to the command chair as a robot slave approached with a silver tray holding a bowl of water and towel. She removed an engagement ring from her finger and threw it onto the tray. She washed the blood from her hand, dried it and waved the slave away.

Seraphine sat down and a second robot slave approached with a silver tray holding a crystal glass and a bottle of champagne. The robot popped open the bottle and filled the glass. After a moment's hesitation, Seraphine picked it up. The slave retreated.

In the viewscreen a nuclear flash appeared on the surface of the planet. Slowly, more and more flashes appeared adjacent to the first flash. A nuclear firestorm began to gradually spread over the world, a creeping wall of fire and death, taking its time to devour the planet.

Seraphine sipped champagne, defeated.

The communication chime sounded.

"What is it?"

The communication officer said, "Incoming transmission, Captain. We've been ordered to remain on station to observe the extermination of this world."

"Yes, of course," she said. "Why not?"

Seraphine threw the glass against the wall, shattering it. Getting up, she retrieved the bottle of champagne. Avoiding the viewscreen, she went around to the back of the command chair, drinking from the bottle. Sitting down on the floor, she began to cry.

* * *

3234 A.D. — YEAR OF THE WOOD TIGER (PRESENT DAY)
SOUTHERN ASTERISMS — PHI 1 PAVONIS / ARCHON

A medical bot hovered over Seraphine, its mechanical arm extended over her head with a medical device in hand. A light touched her forehead, instantly healing the wound. She sat up and spied Sebastian standing next to the medical bot.

"What did you do?" he asked.

"Hmm?" She was still a bit foggy. "Oh, I modified the quantum gravity resonance coil on a hovercar."

"That's extremely dangerous."

"Really?" Seraphine looked directly into his eyes. "Back on Eleutheria, the computer informed me that you had a call from a Free Imperial Knight, a woman named Celestine Ney."

Sebastian was silent.

"Why didn't you betray me?"

"She wasn't paying enough."

"What will you do when you get a better offer?"

Sebastian smiled.

Seraphine sighed. "Tell me what's happened."

"All of the crew are back on the Lethe, captain. Imperial warships are blockading this system. I've activated the Lethe's stealth mode. We're in orbit over Archon."

"Where's Alice?"

"Captain White has returned to her starship," said Sebastian. "The Queen of Diamonds has sailed away, laden with crimes and the riches of Archon."

*   *   *

CHAPTER NINE

A Bed of Sunshine

SOUTHERN ASTERISMS — PHI 1 PAVONIS / ARCHON

Alice lounged in her command chair, one boot propped against the console, her fingers turning the crystal sphere slowly in her palm. Around her, the crew moved with quiet purpose, bathed in the bluish light of the rising planet on the viewscreen. Archon gleamed below, storm washed, ancient, full of secrets. She tilted her head toward Ingli, who sat nearby. "All this excitement over such a little thing," she murmured. Her eyes drifted down to the ancient planet. "But I see an even greater jewel."

Caesar approached Viktor with a new collar in his fists.

Viktor jerked back. "Get away from me!"

Alice didn't raise her voice. "Leave him. He's earned a place on this starship."

Caesar let out a low growl. The other crew members rose from their seats.

Alice remained silent, backing down.

Shtol moved first, grabbing Viktor and pinning him down with brute ease. Caesar forced the collar around the boy's neck. Metal clicked into place.

At the helm station, Nix didn't turn. Her pale white Ta'Lian skin gleamed like polished bone in the command lights. She kept her eyes on the sensor display. "Captain, the star system is full of imperial warships. I doubt we'll be able to avoid them for long."

Alice leaned back. "Ingli, where did you get that medallion?"

Ingli's eyes lingered on Viktor. There was sympathy there, quiet, unsettled. She turned her gaze toward Alice, and she wasn't evasive this time. "I found it on the wreck of a starship which had crashed on my world long ago."

Alice lifted the crystal toward the lights overhead. It caught the glow and fractured it into dozens of tiny suns. "Do you know what information is contained on this crystal?"

Ingli was silent.

Alice gave a faint smile. "I wonder if its worth dying for?"

Shtol interrupted Alice's musings. "Man 'o war, captain. She's got the wind of us. We can't outrun her."

Alice didn't bother to sit up. In a lazy tone, she said, "Guns at the ready."

Caesar turned, disbelief flickering in his eyes. "She outclasses us, captain."

Alice's voice turned sing-song, almost sweet. "Don't you want to play, Caesar?"

A slow grin spread across his face. "Aye, captain." He glanced down at his console. "Our guns are armed and ready."

Alice smiled. "Shtol, hard a port. Caesar, give 'em a taste."

* * *

A yellow star appeared from behind Archon. Rising from the planet's shadow, *The Queen of Diamonds* sailed away into space.

The *Persephone* gave chase.

The Queen of Diamonds turned suddenly and fired a broadside of laser bolts at their pursuer. Crimson light pulses stitched across space. The laser bolts clipped the solar sails of the *Persephone*. One of masts sheared off at the top, sending a cloud of broken debris trailing behind like sparks from a dying fire.

The Imperial starship turned to expose their broadside while *The Queen of Diamonds* twisted away again, vanishing into the dark.

* * *

On the quarterdeck of *The Queen of Diamonds*, Shtol stood

187

at the display, silent, his skin shimmering. "She's turning to fire, captain."

Caesar's tail twitched once. His amber eyes narrowed. "Seventy-four guns. I wonder if we'll survive?"

"Fiddlesticks," Alice said cheerfully, dangling one leg over the arm of her chair. "Nix, extend our hypersails. Let's slip into the vortex before she decides to breathe on us."

The Ta'Lian hesitated. She knew the dangers of entering hyperspace inside the astrosphere of a star as well as anyone. For a heartbeat, her ivory fingers hovered above the controls, motionless. She glanced at Alice.

Alice returned her stare with a wall of dreamy steel. *She won't argue. She never does.*

Nix nodded. "Aye, aye, captain."

Alice smiled and put on a child's expression, all innocence. "I'm feeling lucky."

With a sigh, Nix asked, conversationally, "What course shall I set, captain?"

"Take us to Colony Seven."

Nix nodded. "Aye, aye, captain. Course is set for CD27 14659." Nix closed her eyes and concentrated on the distant star. An instant later, she began to sing. The music was transferred to the cathedral chamber at the fore, and the crystals lining of the hyper

188

sails vibrated in response to her melody.

While listening to Nix's pretty song, Alice watched the approaching warship with professed disdain. While her expression didn't vary, she gripped the armrest, feeling her fingers tighten, just slightly.

Nix stopped singing and waved a hand. The solar sails retracted. She waved a hand again and the hypersails extended into space, unfurling like wings of shimmering glass.

Alice glanced over her shoulder, her voice absent and casual. "Ingli, have you ever met a man named Sebastian?"

Ingli, staring at the holographic display hovering over the binnacle, turned to face Alice. "Yes, he was a prisoner on the Persephone. They thought he was a spy. Now he's the gunner on the Lethe. Why do you ask?"

Alice shrugged, all innocence. "No reason." she leaned forward to brush dirt off her skirt as if it mattered. "Shtol, take us away."

The Sakle alien nodded. "Aye, aye, captain."

* * *

As *The Queen of Diamonds* sailed towards the invisible energy barrier at the edge of the astrosphere, the pull of the hyperspace vortex began to take hold. There was a silent flash, and the starship ground to a halt. All nine of its masts holding the hypersails were torn away. The mandala wormhole collapsed into a chaotic swirl of energy and vanished.

The starship spun aimlessly, dismasted and immobilized, its momentum carrying it in wild, erratic circles. Dead in space, it twirled helplessly—like a child's top spinning without purpose, caught in the whims of fate. They were dead in space, twirling around and around and around.

The *Persephone* sailed out to meet its prey.

* * *

The *Lethe* sailed away from Archon. Far below, the sphere of distorted spacetime, a mere speck on the surface of the planet, shimmered like a diamond in the sunshine.

Seraphine and Sebastian stepped onto the quarterdeck. She lowered herself into a chair with the elegance of habit, her eyes finding Christian across the deck. Her eyes settled on him, cold and steady.

On the main viewscreen, the planet hung in silence, its cities overgrown with greenery. A holographic image hovering over the binnacle displayed *The Queen of Diamonds* at the edge of the star system. The *Persephone* approached like a hound closing in on a wounded bird.

Seraphine shook her head, bewildered. "How can the Imperium know of this world?" She activated the intercom. "What's happening?"

Gisele's voice came over the channel. "Captain White tried to jump to hyperspace too soon." A moment later, the starsinger emerged from the cathedral and made her way aft. "Her starship has been dismasted."

"All nine masts?" asked Seraphine.

Gisele settled into a seat next to Seraphine and nodded.

Christian muttered, "Those that die'll be the lucky ones."

Gisele activated a holographic image of the astrospheric current sheet for Phi 1 Pavonis. The hologram was littered with little lights. With a motion, she enlarged one for analysis. It was a compact, spherical device three meters in diameter. Its surface was composed of matte black alloy, interspersed with hexagonal panels that housed micro-gravitational emitters. Gisele sighed and leaned back in her chair. "Captain, I've detected the presence of a network of gravity resonance mines throughout this star system."

"Can you disable them if we get too close?"

"Certainly, yes."

A dark smile crept into Sebastian's face. "The hunter always wins.'

Seraphine stared at Sebastian. He met her gaze with empty eyes. For the first time, she wondered about his past. "Not always." She broke contact and turned her attention back to Gisele. "Miss Ellestad, take us to the astropause. Set course for HR 8501 and

191

extend the hyper sails. Take us to Bharata."

"Aye, aye, captain."

*   *   *

Dominic walked down a passageway towards the cell where Captain Alice White was held. Through the transparent walls *The Queen of Diamonds*, sans hyper sails, could be seen drifting in space.

Alice watched him approach. Her tone was mocking, childlike. "He came to rescue us, he did. But why did he put me in this cell? And where are my friends?"

Dominic stopped just outside the energy barrier that sealed the cell. "Why do you waste your time with such baseborn life forms?"

She said nothing.

He sighed. "The fate of inferiors is the least of your worries, Captain."

In a dreamy voice, Alice spoke to herself. "He won't tell me where my crew is. Did they all fall down a hole?"

Dominic looked down at her. "As inferiors, they're guilty until proven innocent, but I have chosen to show mercy. I've left them on what remains of your starship."

Alice turned, meeting his eyes. For an instant, he sensed a cold, calculating intelligence there. "They'll all die without help, but you know that, don't you?"

Dominic shrugged. "Their fates are inconsequential."

"Where is the human from my crew?" she asked. "What have you done with Viktor?

"Unlike you, the boy has not been charged with a crime."

"What about Ingli?"

"The girl is with me as well."

Alice dropped her eyes to stare at the wall, muttering to herself. "He thinks I'm a criminal. What have I done out here in space?"

His laughter pulled her attention back. "You have a reputation, Captain White. You're wanted for piracy in twenty-nine star systems. But you will not be summarily executed."

She didn't look at him. "He is so kind, he is."

"You will be sent to Novus Constantinople to stand trial," he remarked. He turned away, walked a few steps, then paused and glanced back at her. "Since you've chosen to associate with deficient minded aliens, there is some doubt as to your sanity. You might not even be given the death penalty."

Alice looked though the transparent wall at her broken starship where her crew was.

Dominic hummed a cheerful tune as he went down the passageway and out the door.

* * *

The main deck of the *Lethe* was quiet. Most of the crew were up in the sails or below decks. Seraphine checked her thunderbolt baton and whispered, "Who dares defy the omnipotent to arms?"

Her voice carried the edge of a dare—and a memory.

With a flick of her wrist, the thunderbolt changed into a spear, and then a sword. She retracted it and attached it to her belt.

Christian entered and leaned against a beam, arms folded. "What are you doing?"

Seraphine walked up to a locker and withdrew a form fitting space suit. As she slipped it on, her voice cut sharp and cold. "You're the first officer of the Lethe and you've been treated handsomely. Now you're nothing but a mutineer, so you can go hang!"

Christian's gaze softened for a split second—an expression that made her pause before she turned away.

What was that look?

She refused to dwell on it. *There's no time for this.*

"Come on, captain. You know I wasn't going to shoot you."

She crossed the deck to the weapons locker, a crooked smile playing at the corner of her mouth. "You and your impulses," she said, almost playfully—but the levity didn't last.

She pulled a laser pistol from the rack, then a particle beam rifle. The smile faded as she checked the rifle's settings. Her hands moved with practiced precision, ghosts of old habits guiding them through motions drilled into her long before she became a pirate. "You broke the code. The only reason I haven't marooned you on

Archon is because I need a good Sail Master"

She reached for a magazine of energized atomic particles and slid it into the rifle with a clean, satisfying click.

"Nilay isn't as good as you are."

Christian came up behind her and placed his hands on her shoulders. "I'm the one who found you on Archon. Did you know that?"

Why does he keep doing this?

She froze, anger rose in her chest, but then it softened, too, just a little. His hands were always so sure.

He's too close.

Seraphine shrugged him off and picked up a bandolier, looping it across her chest. Her voice was low now, bitter. "If you hadn't pointed your weapon at me, we might still have the data crystal. Now, Alice has it. You know what that means?"

She slung the rifle across her back.

"Ingli will use whatever weapon she discovers against the Earth."

Christian took a step back. 'Taint much good for them now, is it? They've been captured."

Seraphine shook her head. "The last thing the Imperium needs is another super weapon."

He studied her face. "No, there is more to it than that. What did you do before you became a pirate? You told Alice you were a Watcher. The captain of a scout ship. You're the one that discovered Iounn, Ingli's homeworld, aren't you?"

She refused to look into his eyes, afraid of what he might see there.

"You destroyed it, didn't you?" he said, voice low. "Trying to atone for your sins?"

She tried to push past him but he wouldn't budge.

"You think you can make up for what you've done through piracy?" Christian stepped back and laughed. "You're crazier than Alice."

Seraphine's gaze drifted past him, and for a moment, the world around her disappeared, like a tide retreating from shore. Laughter rose from the deep, a chorus of children's voices, high and golden, skipping like stones across sunlit water. The faces of children came flooding back, uninvited. They were playing in the sun, full of innocence and light.

It was the last time she had seen them.

The last time anyone saw them.

A single thought surfaced, quiet and cold.

I killed them.

Seraphine shook her head, as if the motion could scatter the memories away. A whisper came, uninvited. "It's just that I can't

196

stop thinking about what I've done."

"You need to let it go."

"Can't."

She pushed past him. He didn't stop her this time.

"I owe Ingli and her people, wherever they are."

She picked up her helmet, its surface dull, as if it, too, remembered, and walked over to the airlock.

Christian stepped into her path. "There's nothing out there but empty space, Captain. Where are you going?"

She looked beyond him, past the airlock, out to the waiting stars. "Out there," she said, "into the never never."

Their eyes met, and for a moment, she had the impulse to remain there, inside those clear blue eyes, a place where she could learn to love again.

He loves me. The thought came to her so quickly, she almost couldn't stop it. *He loves me.* Denial stirred within her, like a storm gathering strength, determined to drown the thought before it could fully take hold. *How can he?* The question spun through her mind. *How long has he carried these feelings?* Mentally, she shook her head. *No, it's too late for that.*

The cold crept back into her bones.

"Out of my way, Christian."

He stepped aside and Seraphine entered the airlock.

He shouted after her. "Go then—and be damned t'ye wi' all my heart!"

The door hissed shut.

He slammed his fist against the glass. "I'm telling you, this'll be a bloody end to everything! Go on, then. Be off to hell!"

Through the airlock window, he watched as she turned her back on him.

The deck fell quiet again.

Christian stood there for a moment, like a shadow in a room without light.

She was gone.

He wanted to activate his communicator, to call after her, to ask her to stay, but the words never came.

In the glass of the airlock, Christian saw Gisele's reflection. "Why didn't you shoot me on Archon?"

Gisele smiled. "Greed never wins out over love."

Through the glass of the airlock door, Christian watched Seraphine exit the *Lethe*, stepping out into empty space.

He turned to look at Gisele. "If you ever point a laser at me again, I'll kill you."

Gisele smiled. "If you ever do something that requires me to point a laser at you, I won't hesitate to shoot."

*   *   *

Dominic marched onto the star deck of the *Persephone*, his boots striking the floor with the cold rhythm of authority. The air was taught, waiting. Captain Septimus Flavius stood on the quarterdeck next to the helm officer.

"Captain Flavius," Dominic said. "Have the starsinger tune the hypersails for the long journey home."

"What course, sir?"

"Alpha Mensae," he said. It was the star that warmed the capitol of the Imperium. Novus Constantinople. "Have the rest of the legion remain here to guard Archon. Procuratores Centenarii Malakar will remain in command."

"Aye, aye, sir."

Silence descended over the star deck, a brief stillness like the moment before glass breaks.

There was a distant flash at the edge of the star system. A petal of white fire opened against the black. An officer leaned toward the nearest holographic array, fingers brushing the controls. "Captain, a starship has struck one of our gravity mines."

A faint smile curved across Dominic's face, slow as an eclipse. He stepped closer to the hologram, eyes fixed on the dying spark. "Captain Flavius," he said without turning, "have the starsinger tune the hypersails to match Alpha Mensae, but do not enter the vortex yet. Take us to that starship."

"Aye, aye, sir."

* * *

A gravity well surrounded the *Lethe*, which drifted, dead in space. As the *Persephone* approached, a figure in a space suit surrounded by an energy shield fired maneuvering jets and was propelled towards the man 'o war. The shield glowed red just before the figure struck the hull, burning through it. A blue energy barrier sealed the hole in the spaceship after the figure passed through the hull.

Two more figures, surrounded by shields, appeared. Following the first figure, they struck the hull of the *Persephone* and burned through the hull. As the Persephone came close to it's prey, the gravity well faded away suddenly. The *Lethe* fired thrusters and shot away into space, escaping.

* * *

Seraphine stood in a long corridor illuminated by the blue forcefield that held off the vacuum of space. With the touch of a button, her helmet disappeared into a pocket dimension. She raised her particle beam rifle and moved off down the corridor. A warbot appeared at one end of the corridor. She shot it before it could fire. She walked past the smoking ruins of the war machine and deeper into the starship.

On the star deck of the *Persephone*, Dominic and Captain Flavius stood in silence, watching the retreating *Lethe* shrink into the darkness. Its glow pulsed like a dying ember slipping through the fingers of fate.

Flavius broke the silence, his voice as measured as a chronometer. "They've used enough fuel to burn out a sunstone. Should we pursue?"

Before Dominic could respond, a chime cut through the moment, followed by a technician's voice over the comm channel. "Sir, there has been a hull breech on deck sixteen. There are reports of weapons fire."

Flavius straightened. "Alert the crew. Have security bots secure the area."

"Aye, aye, sir."

* * *

Seraphine moved through the dim passageways of the *Persephone*, her footsteps silent over the metal decking. Anyone who crossed her path dropped in a flash of white light—stunned by her laser pistol. Security drones met harsher ends; her particle beam rifle carved through their metal bodies light lightning through brittle stone.

A security bot came into view and fired. The laser beam struck her energy shield, overloading it with a brief flare of crimson. She ducked, letting the beam burn past, and rolled behind a support strut. A flick of her thumb adjusted the rifle's settings. She stepped out and fired, one clean shot. The beam punched through the robot's defenses, and the machine erupted in a hiss of sparks and smoke.

Without warning, two rings along the wall glowed red and vanished in a fiery display, punching a pair of holes in the hull. Two shielded figures stepped through the molten edges, leaving shimmering energy membranes behind to patch the breach.

Christian. Sebastian.

Seraphine's jaw tightened. "What are you doing here?"

Sebastian flashed a grin that didn't reach his eyes. "Hunting, captain."

He didn't wait for her reply. He turned and sprinted in the opposite direction. Christian paused just long enough to offer a shrug, then followed.

Seraphine exhaled sharply and ran after them.

They reached the cell block moments later. Sebastian veered toward one of the cells and halted. With a gesture, the barrier dissolved, vanishing like mist.

Alice stood inside.

Seraphine caught up and shoved Sebastian hard against the wall. "You came here to help her? After what she did?"

"They're going to execute her."

Seraphine let go of him and took a step back. "What's she to you?"

Seraphine didn't answer. For the first time, the lost expression in his eyes had faded away. There was something else there now. Warmth and determination mingled together.

Was it love?

Alice's voice cut in. "Forget about me. Save my crew."

Seraphine glanced at Alice. "What? They're only aliens."

"They're my friends!"

Seraphine drew a blaster pistol and held it out to Alice. "Help them yourself."

Alice took the blaster and they stepped out of the cell.

Christian ran over to meet them. "There's no way out that way."

A moment later, several security bots appeared, blocking their escape.

Alice shot the first one that stepped into the corridor. "What a rescue!"

They withdrew back into the cell just as a dozen laser bolts flew past them.

Seraphine pointed her particle beam rifle down at the deck and fired.

The impact hit like a hammer out of the underworld. Metal

warped and screamed. Smoke spilled upward as the burst of energized atomic particles tore through the plating.

A blackened hole yawned open beneath them.

Heat blasted their faces. For a heartbeat, it felt like the starship itself was on fire.

They jumped.

*   *   *

At the aft of the *Persephone*, windows peered out at the stars from the captain's stateroom. A mahogany table rested in the center of the cabin between a large four-poster bed and a desk that held a computer terminal. A holographic star chart was suspended over the desk, centered on the local star, Phi 1 Pavonis.

Ingli Nivienne sat by the window, gazing out at the stars. Around her ankle was an iron ring attached to a chain that was affixed to the wall.

Viktor sat in a chair in the corner, hugging his knees.

The door disintegrated in molten fire and a moment later Seraphine stepped through, followed by Christian, Alice and Sebastian. Viktor rose quickly and rushed to Alice, who rebuffed his embrace.

Ingli glanced at them briefly, then turned back to the stars.

Seraphine walked up to Ingli and said, "Where is it?"

Ingli didn't look at her. "The stars are such a lonely sight. My world is no longer out there, is it?"

"The crystal sphere from Archon," said Seraphine. "Tell me where it is."

Ingli pointed toward the desk.

The crystal sat in plain view.

Seraphine retrieved it, holding it up to the light with a crooked smile. "Well, that was easy," she said softly, a spark of mischief flickering beneath the weariness in her eyes. "Almost makes you wonder what the catch is."

She lowered the sphere, her fingers tightening just slightly, as if she expected it to vanish.

It didn't.

Seraphine looked at Ingli and the spark of mischief faded away with her smile.

"I used to hike a mountain trail around a lake on my world," Ingli said. "In spring, the fields were always full of beautiful flowers."

Seraphine glanced at the others. Her fingers felt cold around the crystal.

This isn't the time.

Ingli continued, "One day, there was a terrific rush of wind and a noise like thunder. The biggest thing that ever was, grotesque and beautiful, appeared out of a flash of light. It was an immense pillar of fire. I thought a god had crashed into the sun."

Seraphine looked away from Ingli and out at the stars, wishing she could hide there in the darkness.

"Then there was another flash. And another. And another. And another."

Seraphine closed her eyes.

Ingli's quiet voice penetrated the darkness. "The blue horizon turned into a firestorm."

Opening her eyes, Seraphine drew a hand laser and burned through the chain. The metal fell away, releasing Ingli.

"Come with us."

Ingli didn't move. "Now, all of the flowers are gone."

Seraphine didn't have anything else to say. She stood there, silent.

Viktor came over and took Ingli's hand.

The touch brought Ingli back to the present. She was only a lost girl, all alone.

Alice whispered, "Please come with us."

Ingli nodded and stood. She followed them out.

The holographic star chart flickered and faded away.

* * *

A pair of security robots stood guard by the landing bay, their rigid frames gleaming under the cold white glow of overhead lights. When movement stirred at the far end of the corridor, their optics flared. Weapons lifted in unison. The first laser bolts streaked through the air, along with the zrak-boom sounds of blaster fire.

Flashes from energy shields lit up the corridor. Seraphine dove out of the firestorm just as her shield spluttered and went out with a dying hiss. Peering around the edge of a wall, she raised her particle beam rifle and fired. As the beam struck the robots—bright flares erupted where they stood as they disintegrated into blinding light.

Seraphine waved her companions forward. Sebastian, Alice and Viktor ran into the landing bay and sprinted toward a small cutter, but Ingli let go of Alice's hand, remaining out in the open. Her face was full of bewilderment.

Christian didn't hesitate. He broke cover, collided with Ingli, and shoved her down behind a support column just as reinforcements poured into the corridor.

A dozen soldiers in black armor entered with practiced precision, followed by heavy warbots. They surrounded Christian.

He didn't resist.

A warbot pushed him to his knees and restraints locked around his wrists.

Silence fell over the landing bay.

Seraphine closed her eyes, unwilling to watch them drag Christian away.

When she looked again, Ingli stood nearby, watching her.

Seraphine swallowed hard. "Ingli, I commanded the starship that discovered your planet, Iounn."

Ingli didn't reply.

"I destroyed your world."

The silence lingered.

Confusion mixed with disbelief in Ingli's face. Her voice, when it came, carried no anger—only sadness. "How could you do such a thing?"

Seraphine was unable to answer.

"My people are dead. My world is gone. I am alone."

A voice rang out, sharp and cold. "Taking credit for my accomplishments Seraphine?"

Dominic stepped into view, flanked by security robots. The light caught the angles of his face as if he had been sculpted from ambition. Inanna walked beside him, graceful and silent, her gaze passing over Seraphine like she wasn't there.

Seraphine turned from Ingli and faced him. "I was the captain of the Brandywine. I'm responsible."

"You?" he laughed. "You had nothing to do with it!"

He looked at Ingli. "But you're not the only one left, are you Ingli? How did you survive?"

Ingli remained silent.

Ignoring Inanna by his side, Dominic turned back to Seraphine, his voice softening. "Why not stay here with me? There are still countless worlds to conquer. Fulfill your destiny."

Seraphine's eyes went cold. "I'll never serve them again."

Dominic shook his head and looked at Ingli. "Is it her?" he asked. "Is your conscience bothering you because they look like us?"

Seraphine didn't answer.

He reached out, and a soldier handed him a laser rifle. He turned it over in his hands like it was something sacred. "Let me show you how unimportant they are."

He raised the rifle and aimed it at Ingli.

Seraphine stepped between them. "No!"

The pulse of laser light struck her squarely in the chest. The energy pulse lit up the bay. Her body folded, silent, and dropped. The data crystal slipped from her pocket and rolled across the floor into the shadows.

Ingli stood frozen for a moment, then ran—panic overtaking her.

Inanna stepped backward, vanishing into the corridor like a cat avoiding a falling vase.

Christian shouted and fought against his restraints. He tried to get up, but a soldier slammed him back down to the deck.

While they were distracted, Ingli darted for the cutter. Alice reached out and pulled her aboard. Moments later, the ship rose, its engines flaring to life. It slipped through the energy field protecting the landing bay and vanished into space.

Dominic dropped to his knees beside Seraphine, gathering her into his arms.

Christian's cries echoed across the landing bay, then tumbled into quiet sobs.

*   *   *

Silence pressed down on the medical bay of the *Persephone*. Monitors pulsed in soft blue tones, casting shifting shadows on the walls. A healer stood by the bio-bed where Seraphine lay, his hands over her wound, which slowly regenerated while he concentrated.

Dominic stood a few paces away, folding thin squares of origami paper into little stars—each crease precise, deliberate. He moved without sound, save for the faint rustle of paper. One by one, the stars dropped into a clear glass container beside the bed. Their colorful shapes piled up in silence.

Dominic watched the healer work without truly seeing him. "Long ago, when we were exploring out on the frontiers of the Imperium, I gave Seraphine a present."

Another star took shape between his fingers.

"When she opened the box, half a dozen chocolates lay inside on a bed of sunshine."

He folded one more star, and dropped it into the glass. The

container was full now. He placed a wooden lid on top and let his hand linger on the grain of the surface.

"When she saw them," he continued, "a smile lit up her face."

A warm smile came to his face as he paused in remembrance.

"It was the happiest day of my life."

The healer finished working on Seraphine. He stepped away from the bio-bed.

"She will need to rest awhile," he said, placing a hand gently on Dominic's shoulder.

Taking a deep breath, Dominic nodded. "Thank you, healer."

The man left without another word.

He was alone again.

Dominic turned back to the bio-bed. She lay there, as beautiful as the stars. He took Seraphine's hand in his. Her skin was cold.

Her hand stirred—barely—and closed around his, like a flower beginning to open in the dark. Her eyes fluttered open, slow and uncertain.

He didn't move. Didn't speak.

A shadow of a smile came.

Then, softly, she squeezed his hand.

* * *

CHAPTER TEN
The Kiss

SOUTHERN ASTERISMS — PHI 1 PAVONIS / ARCHON

Dominic stood next to Seraphine on the command deck, eyes fixed on the transparent dome overhead. The force-field shimmered faintly, and beyond was the darkness of the void, sprinkled with stars. Phi 1 Pavonis was a small disk of white light in the distance. The wreck of *The Queen of Diamonds* drifted inside the astropause like a crown sinking into dark water. One cohort of a thousand starships approached the *Persephone*, while the rest of the legion remained to guard the prize Archon.

From behind them, Inanna stood quiet as a shadow.

Dominic spoke. "You know, in ancient times, humans were just one of the animals. If you're strong, you win. If you're weak, you lose. Nature has always been a kill or be killed system. There's no such thing as morality in the wilderness of the universe. The weak will always be abused. It is only the strong who are feared."

Seraphine didn't reply—didn't look at him at all. She stood there, silently watching the ancient light of Phi 1 Pavonis as it warmed the homeworld of the Archons. It was like any other star—steady, heartless. Somewhere down there, the planet turned, cradling a wilderness full of deserted cities.

A soft chime preceded the communications officer's voice. "Legatus, we've contacted the First Citizen through the hyperspace communication crystal, as you requested."

Dominic straightened up slightly. "Brilliant. Put him on."

A holographic viewscreen appeared. The image of the First Citizen, Leopold Voss dominated the screen. He was standing on the command deck of *The Royal Sovereign*, the slowly turning planet Tuathe filling the view behind him. Debris filled the silence above the planet. Alien warships torn open and adrift, like broken toys scattered after the play turned violent.

Leopold's gaze found Seraphine, but his words were for Dominic. "Legatus."

Dominic stepped forward, eager. "Greetings, Citizen. I have good news. This here is—"

"Seraphine DeVere," Leopold interrupted. "Yes, I remember. I awarded you the Imperial Starburst. You eliminated a menace from the planet Iounn."

Seraphine shook her head. "They were never a threat to us."

"Your official report indicated otherwise," said Leopold.

Silence descended over the star deck.

Dominic held up the crystal which Captain White had procured from the ancient planet. "I have recovered this from Archon. I believe it contains the plans for advanced weapons of mass destruction."

Leopold's hard expression softened. "Excellent! We've run out of Archon bombs," he said. "Conquering Tauthe has been difficult. Casualty reports are high. That data crystal will save a lot of human lives, Legatus."

Seraphine watched Dominic, who seemed to be mustering the courage to say something.

Noticing, Leopold raised an eyebrow. "What is it?"

Dominic took a breath. "I have a request, sir."

"Yes?"

"I would like Seraphine DeVere reinstated as a centurion."

Seraphine's voice came before she could stop it. "What?"

Leopold's gaze hardened. "Piracy and treason are serious crimes. You want me to grant her a full pardon?"

Dominic nodded. "Yes, sir. Without DeVere's help, we wouldn't have acquired this data crystal from Archon."

Leopold exhaled slowly, like a man indulging in something he knew he shouldn't. "You're asking a great deal, Legatus."

"I know, sir."

Leopold studied Seraphine for a long moment. "I shall consider it. For now, keep her under guard. Allow her to retain her thunderbolt as a remembrance of who she once was."

"Yes, sir."

The signal ended.

Seraphine turned, boots echoing on the command deck as she walked off.

The two security drones followed without sound, trailing her like shadows.

Dominic watched her go.

*   *   *

Inanna stepped up beside Dominic. She didn't look at Seraphine—only at him. "That was a mistake," she said, her tone low and certain. "DeVere is dangerous."

Dominic didn't turn. His gaze remained fixed on the maneuvering starships. "I didn't ask for your opinion."

There was a moment of silence.

Through the transparent dome above the command deck,

Archon loomed—silent, indifferent, godlike, watching, judging. The First Cohort of the 9th Legion had reached its position. The starships slid into formation with mechanical precision, a glittering constellation of steel.

Inanna moved closer, her presence warm and deliberate. Her fingertips brushed the air just short of his, then, like a serpent circling its prey, her hand found his—slow, almost tender.

Her voice was a whispered invitation. "Who do you desire?"

Dominic knocked her hand away.

Without another word, he followed Seraphine off the command deck.

Inanna remained where she was, simmering in silence.

* * *

Seraphine entered the observation lounge and paused in front of the immense transparent wall that offered a view of the stars.

A pair of security robots stood motionless at each end of the room. Their armored exteriors glinted in the light, and their glowing blue optics scanned every corner with unblinking precision. Hovering just above the deck, they seemed to be little more than metal statues—silent, watching. Their presence hung over the room like a storm cloud, ever present, heavy with the threat of what they might do if called upon.

Dominic entered and came up behind her.

She couldn't bring herself to look at him. "When we returned from HD 154088, I thought they'd imprison us for our mistake."

HD 154088 was the star that once warmed Ingli's home, Iounn. Seraphine was unable to utter the name of the planet which they had destroyed. She remembered the First Citizen's admiring look as he pinned the Imperial Starburst on her uniform.

"I tried to protect you, to take all the blame," she whispered. "But they gave me a medal."

Dominic's voice ignited into hot coals. "You stole the credit," he said. "It was mine and mine alone."

She turned to face him. "Is that what you believe?"

His voice died down to a smoldering cinder. "It doesn't matter anymore, Seraphine."

An unanswered question lingered. *How did you turn into a monster?* Another question emerged, accusing: *How could I have ever loved you?*

She shook her head. "I can't let you keep it, Dominic. I have to destroy the crystal."

He looked at her, taken aback. "Why? You can have your old life back," he said. "No more crazy adventures."

Her gaze fell down to the cold hard deck. "Why did you kill them all?"

Dominic flinched, took a step back, and turned away from her.

"You've forgotten. You don't remember what it was like on Earth after the war."

Seraphine closed her eyes against the pain.

The memory of her childhood came to her in fragments: the crumbling streets, the stench of ash and burnt flesh, the silence that came after the bombs. Her hands, small and quick, darting through rusted metal and broken glass in search of food. Every day, she hid in forgotten corners, watching the shadows of strangers drift past, learning to be silent, to be unseen.

Once, a boy had torn a piece of bread from her hands, knocked her to the ground, and left her bleeding. His laughter hurt more than the blow. It was the same lesson she'd learned again and again—from different mouths, in different forms: only the strong survive.

It wasn't just the boy in the ruins. It was the centurions who trained her, the officers who praised brutality, the speeches that called mercy a weakness. It was a society shaped by survival, forged in fear, and hardened into conquest. She had grown up in it, was shaped by it—and sometimes, she feared it still lived inside her.

In the silence of the ruined city, her only companions were hunger, and the dreams of a life she would never know.

Dominic's words shattered the quiet of her thoughts: "You've forgiven."

Her hand tightened into a fist at her side.

No.

Opening her eyes again, Seraphine looked at the stars outside the immense window. They were like distant embers, trapped behind a pane of glass. "I remember it still," she whispered, "but the natives of Iounn were not dangerous."

From somewhere, the rhythmic cadence of marching boots approached.

* * *

3232 A.D. — YEAR OF THE WATER RAT (TWO YEARS AGO) AZURE DRAGON OF THE EAST — HD 154088 / IOUNN

Lieutenant Dominic Fontaine marched towards the airlock of the launch from the *Brandywine*, flanked by a contingent of imperial soldiers. As he reached the door, he activated the viewscreen.

A lush field of grass, dotted with wildflowers, stretched toward the horizon. A group of Iounnian natives stood near a waterfall, saying their farewells to the departing human visitors. An extremely attractive man embraced Seraphine and kissed her passionately, while other humans exchanged similar gestures of affection. The team of contact scientists walked toward the airlock of the launch, their voices raised in light conversation.

The space inside Dominic's heart collapsed into a void that swallowed everything. The fires that followed were slow and insidious, leaving only hollow ash and the pale remains of a love snuffed out in silence.

*   *   *

3234 A.D. — YEAR OF THE WOOD TIGER (PRESENT DAY)
SOUTHERN ASTERISMS — PHI 1 PAVONIS / ARCHON

Seraphine stood before the windows, gazing out at the stars surrounding Archon.

Behind her, Dominic's presence was a quiet weight. His voice, low and warm, brushed against her ear. "When you were leaving Iounn, I saw you in the viewscreen."

Feeling his breath on her neck, she had an impulse to give in to it. Her response was full of distracted innocence. "Mm?"

"I saw you kiss one of the Iounnians."

The shock of it struck her like a thunderbolt. She felt an urge to run far, far away, to hide in a cave and never come out. He had seen one of the natives kiss her. *What was his name? Kyros. The most beautiful man I have ever known.* The air around her tightened as the memory struck—a soft kiss, the warmth of it against the backdrop of a garden paradise.

Her eyes fluttered shut. "How could you? An entire planet—"

His voice broke the silence, raw and distant, like a bird's cry in a vast, empty sky. "I am what you've made me, Seraphine. But it's much more than that. I thought of what was happening to me, the pain of losing you, and I realized how the people of Iounn would affect the rest of humanity. It was unbearable to imagine."

She opened her eyes and looked at his reflection in the glass. "So you killed them all."

"I would do anything for the Earth," he said. "I would do anything for you."

Dominic kissed her on the shoulder.

Seraphine whirled around. "Get away from me!"

She pushed him away, the force of it surprising even her.

Her voice, low and steady, carried the weight of a decision made in the quiet spaces of her mind, far from this moment. "The universe is full of pain, Dominic. But I will no longer contribute to the misery of others, no matter who they are."

Her hand dropped to her belt, where the Vajra Thunderbolt waited. As she drew it, the baton transformed into a flaming sword. "I'm taking the crystal sphere."

His gaze turned cold, like a storm cloud rolling across a quiet sky. He drew his Vajra Thunderbolt and it transformed into a spear. Electricity danced along its length. He smiled without warmth. "You'll have to kill me to get it."

With an anguished cry, she struck.

Dominic blocked her attack and lunged at her while electricity danced along the shaft.

She knocked the spear aside and counterattacked.

He jumped out of the way.

Fire and lightning swirled around each other in a beautiful dance. Her breath came fast, each strike met with an effortless parry. He was incredibly fast, quicker than she remembered. She paused, eyes narrowing. "What's this?"

The security robots moved forward but he waved them back. It was a casual gesture that made her wonder. "You can't beat me in a fight, Seraphine."

Her lips parted, and she blinked in disbelief. "You—" she didn't want to say it, "—you have been enhanced?"

Dominic nodded. "Yes. Now, I'm stronger and quicker than you will ever be."

A cold shiver went down her spine, and for a moment, her knees felt weak. "But you'll die," she whispered. "Age regression kills enhanced humans."

"I have become great, Seraphine. You can't fight me."

Seraphine took a few breaths and determination brought back her strength. She threw a flurry of sword strikes at him, but the spear was always there, blocking, parrying.

He moved with effortless precision, too quick for her to anticipate. Each time she attacked, he was there, like an immovable wall. She spun trying to catch him off guard, but he was already moving again.

A smirk tugged at his lips, as if the entire fight were little more than a game. He was a cat playing with a mouse. "I've always wondered how Ingli survived. You're helping them. How many more are there?"

Her eyes narrowed in determination. *You will never know.*

Seraphine twirled her Vajra Thunderbolt and it transformed into a laser whip. She advanced, twirling, and became a wall of spinning energy.

He retreated, parrying with his spear but it was struck and it flew out of his hand.

One of the security robots took aim and fired.

Zzrak-boom!

The slug of energized atomic particles struck a console and exploded.

* * *

Seraphine ran out onto the main deck, boots skimming over the steel. A dozen security bots come forward and tried to shoot her with their blasters and lasers, but she whirled out of the way. She spun through the firestorm, her energy whip a streak of light carving through the air. Atomic particles ricocheted off the whirling wall of energy, created as she twirled round and round with the energy whip.

The firestorm paused a moment. The robots had stopped firing, assessing their next move. With a grin, she rushed forward, cutting through the robots in a spinning storm of fury. Machines collapsed around her in a rain of shattered alloy.

With a shout, Dominic re-entered the fight. His thunderbolt had been transformed into a power enhanced mace. He swung at Seraphine but she tumbled out of the way. The mace struck a console and the metal shattered like broken glass.

He struck again.

She leaped out of the way.

The wall behind her disintegrated in a glowing ruin.

The deck shook beneath her. She lost her footing, fell, and rolled onto her back.

His shadow fell over her.

The tip of his thunderbolt, now a spear again, pressed against her chest.

"You'll never be as strong as I am."

* * *

3232 A.D. — YEAR OF THE WATER RAT (TWO YEARS AGO)
AZURE DRAGON OF THE EAST — HD 154088 / IOUNN

Seraphine sat with her back to her command chair on the *Brandywine* while Iounn was displayed on the viewscreen. It was slowly being consumed in a thermonuclear firestorm. For a time, she watched the glow of the fires dance across the rear wall of the star deck. Every flash was another town, gone. It became unbearable to watch. Furious, she got up, went over to a console and entered commands. A moment after, a robot slave entered the star deck. She handed a data crystal to the robot. The slave bowed and went out.

The *Brandywine* remained in orbit while the orange flames slowly crept over the surface. A small starship, the *Fantome*, emerged from the *Brandywine's* hold. Spinning upside down, it dropped down into the atmosphere to land on the planet.

*   *   *

A group of Iounnians stood in a grassy field, watching in horror as the firestorm approached. It crept over the horizon, glowing red, pulsing like the heartbeat of a dying god. No one spoke. No one ran.

The *Fantome* descended without a sound, its shadow slipping over the landscape. It landed on the field silently. The hatch hissed open.

A lone robot stepped out. With a simple gesture, it waved them over.

The Iounnians hesitated. Then, one by one, they moved.

A current of footsteps.

Ingli was among them.

Hundreds of Iounnians vanished inside the ship's narrow body.

The hatch closed.

The *Fantome* lifted off, just as the flash came.

Behind it, the grassy field folded into fire like a book closing on a forgotten memory.

*   *   *

3234 A.D. — YEAR OF THE WOOD TIGER (PRESENT DAY) SOUTHERN ASTERISMS — PHI 1 PAVONIS / ARCHON

On the *Persephone*, Seraphine lay on her back, defeated, staring up at Dominic. The point of the spear hovered just above her chest. She couldn't move. The voice of her mentor, William, came from somewhere: *Compassion is where strength comes from. Not the false strength of brute force, but the true strength of character and heart.*

In an instant, she thought of the Iounnians. Their children. Ingli.

Her hand tightened around the thunderbolt.

Her true strength was something he would never understand.

I can win this.

Dominic grinned above her. "I'm going to find them, Seraphine. The Iounnians. I'm going to kill them all, one by one."

Her knuckles whitened around the weapon.

He tilted his head slightly. "What I don't understand is why you chose inferior aliens over your own people," he said. "I lost you the day you went down to that world."

In one breathless motion, Seraphine transformed her thunderbolt into a short sword and knocked the spear aside. Rolling up, she

227

rose in one fluid movement. She transformed her thunderbolt into a bladed staff and moved forward, throwing a series of quick strikes.

Dominic parried them all, but slipped and fell down onto his back, dropping his weapon.

She hesitated. Love clinging to sorrow.

The truth of what she had to do darkened her heart.

Her vision blurred with the sting of unwanted tears, and though she tried to blink them away, they refused to stop.

"I was always yours, Dominic."

With an anguished cry, she struck.

Clang!

A blade intercepted hers—steel against steel, ringing like a bell at the end of the world.

Light flooded the deck, sharp and blinding.

Dominic rolled clear.

Seraphine stumbled back, eyes narrowing against the glare.

Inanna stood in the center of it, surrounded by an aura of brilliant, shining light.

Dominic retrieved his weapon and rose, squinting. "What's going on, Inanna?"

Her voice came from the light—no longer mortal.

"I am not Inanna," she said. "I am Eiris, Queen of the Archons."

Seraphine's breath caught, her pulse quickening. The words weren't just spoken; they reverberated through the main deck. The air felt heavier, as though it were being pressed down by something ancient and unfathomable, something that had been locked away for an eternity.

Dominic and Seraphine exchanged a glance, their eyes locking for only a heartbeat. A silent understanding passed between them. In that moment they were no longer enemies—pirate against imperial solder. They were allies. Humanity above all.

The light around Eiris bent and twisted, alive with a storm of colors. It was like the sun rising over a shattered world, brilliant and terrible in equal measure.

Seraphine took an instinctive step back. This was not Inanna. This was something else entirely. The woman who had once served at Dominic's side was gone, replaced by something—divine—something untouchable, cold.

Dominic confronted the Queen of Archon. "What have you done with Inanna?"

"Inanna serves me," said Eiris. Her voice carried the weight of a thousand storms. "Just as the Imperium shall serve Archon."

Seraphine felt a tingling sensation creep down her spine.

Archon.

The word hung in the air, ancient and full of promise—and

doom. The Archons were the stuff of legends, whispered of in the darkest corners of the Imperium. Gods that conquered the galaxy, ascended to heaven and were forgotten, their names erased by time. Yet, a woman, Inanna, had been possessed by one. A real Archon stood before them.

Dominic's nod was imperceptible, a subtle gesture toward the exit.

Returning the nod, Seraphine moved silently, slipping back into the shadows.

Dominic reached for the data crystal, tossing it to Seraphine with a swift, practiced motion. She caught it, but her hands were trembling. He was already moving towards Eiris with his Vajra Thunderbolt out. With a swift motion of his hand, he transformed the baton into a flaming spear. He called out over his shoulder. "Go!"

Seraphine hesitated.

The storm broke.

Suddenly, Inanna advanced on Seraphine in a lightning quick attack.

There was a flash of silver and Seraphine found herself on her back, winded and gasping for breath. Before she could react, Dominic was there, his weapon raised in a blur of motion.

The clang of steel rang out as he intercepted the blow meant for Seraphine's head. The sound was harsh, metallic, and resonant. It made her jump.

Seraphine scrambled backward, her heart thundering in her chest. She rose to her feet, eyes locked on Inanna. The woman's body shimmered with an impossibly bright light, as if her skin had been woven from a thousand stars, each one burning with its own intensity. The sight of it stole Seraphine's breath away.

Dominic lunged forward, meeting Eiris' fury with his own. They clashed in a brutal exchange of strikes, each movement crackling with power. Out of the chaos, Seraphine heard Dominic's voice—a desperate command. "Get out of here!"

Seraphine's pulse spiked. Her legs moving before her mind could catch up. As if waking from a dream, she broke into a run, the data crystal clutched tightly in her hand.

Behind her, Eiris' laughter thundered through the deck—distant and fading, swallowed up by the clash of battle.

*   *   *

Eiris moved with the fluidity of a storm, her senses thrumming with the power coursing through Inanna's body. Dominic's strikes were fast—faster than any normal man—but they were still too human, too slow. She parried each blow with effortless grace.

It was quite amusing.

His enhanced strength and speed—his superiority   none of

it mattered in the face of her divinity. She let him fight. Let him believe he could win. His desperation was intoxicating. She allowed him the illusion of struggle, just for fun, drawing him in before she struck.

The moment came and she struck him down.

He lay on the floor, bleeding.

With slow, deliberate grace, she stepped over him, straddling his chest. She leaned down, her expression cool and radiant. "Do you think I would ever let your kind plunder my world?" she said. "You are inferior."

His reaction was a surprise. Bleeding, broken, he smiled up at her with maddening defiance. "Seraphine got away from you."

The smile on her face faltered, just for a moment. She turned her eyes towards the corridor. Eiris went over to a console and with a wave of her hand, turned it on. The screen came to life, revealing a launch slipping away, barely more than a glimmer of light.

A tiny, futile escape.

Eiris lingered there for a moment, watching the speck vanish into darkness. Then, she turned back to say something to Dominic.

But he had faded away.

* * *

Seraphine piloted a launch while gazing at the stars on the viewscreen. She looked down at the Archonian data crystal in her hand and she wondered why Dominic had thrown it to her. A dark emptiness lay against her heart. Was Dominic still alive? In the viewscreen, the *Persephone* shrank away as she made her escape. "Goodbye, Dominic."

*   *   *

3235 A.D. — YEAR OF THE WOOD RABBIT
BLACK TORTOISE OF THE NORTH
GLIESE 783 AB / ELEUTHERIA

The Queen's Revenge rocked gently in the harbor, her masts creaking in the salt-kissed wind. Seabirds wheeled overhead, crying out as they dove toward the water. Waves lapped against the starship's hull in a lazy rhythm. Around her, dozens of starships—some sleek, some patched together with scavenged hulls—rested like weary travelers come to shore.

The ship's bell rang out six times, in sets of two dings each. It was three hours into the morning watch. Across the bay, bells rang out from other starships. It was a music that repeated every half hour.

On the deck, Ingli, Shtol, and Viktor worked through the cargo—loot they had acquired from a recent raid—checking crates and updating manifests.

Ingli crouched beside one particularly large container, her brow furrowed. "More weapons," she muttered. "Warfare. Always warfare.

233

I don't think they realize how powerful they are without it."

Shtol stretched his back and offered a dry smile. "Let's hope they never learn. Humans are enough trouble as they are."

Ingli looked up at the sky and saw another starship coming down from orbit. As it descended, it transformed. Six of the nine masts retracted and the cylindrical hull reshaped into the smooth lines of an ancient sailing vessel. It came down close to the water and halted just a few meters above it. She heard the whine of antigravity engines change, and the starship settled into the bay without a splash. Native Phinians—dolphin-like beings, swam around the starship. A few of them leaped into the air and called out a greeting in their strange language.

Alice glanced up at the flag: A skull with crossed swords underneath, next to a champagne bottle. It was the *Lethe*, Captain DeVere's starship.

A hovercar emerged from the *Lethe* and flew over to The Queen's Revenge.

Caesar called up to Alice, tail flicking. "Captain, we've got a visitor."

Alice put down a computer tablet. "Are we having a party? No one told me."

Caesar laughed and went over to the side to extend a gangplank.

Seraphine stepped out onto the quarterdeck. It had been twen-

234

ty-five solar days since she had sailed away from Archon. Eleutheria was 74.92 light years from the ancient world. It was outside the Imperium altogether. The long voyage gave her time to think.

Alice leaned on the railing of the poop deck and called down to her. "Come to see my new corsair? I've named her, The Queen's Revenge."

Seraphine crossed her arms. "I'd like to speak with Ingli."

Alice waved in Ingli's direction.

Seraphine walked across the quarterdeck. The sea wind tugged loose strands of her hair across her cheek. She found Ingli sitting next to a crate of laser rifles, bound for William Parker, their contact. Ingli looked up at her without saying anything.

Rather than giving them privacy, Shtol remained where he was, counting the rifles and looking sidelong at Seraphine. It was as if he wanted to protect Ingli.

Seraphine held out the crystal sphere from Archon. "I think you should have this."

Ingli looked at it without reaching for it. "Why?"

"You understand these kinds of weapons better than anyone else," said Seraphine.

Ingli took the sphere slowly. She turned it over in her hands and the crystal caught the light of the Gliese 783. For a long moment, she didn't speak. It looked like she was debating whether or not to throw it away, into the harbor. She brushed a strand of hair out of her face and set the crystal down onto a table. "I don't know how to open it."

Alice, now curious, turned to the Ta'Lian woman. "Nix, can you break Archon locks?"

The fairy-like woman had a chalky-white face. Nix smirked. "I can break any lock." With a flutter of her wings, Nix flew over to a staircase that led down below.

Seraphine looked up at Alice, wondering if she was crazy enough to break the code.

The pirates of Eleutheria had an agreement. The planet was neutral territory. No fighting. William enforced this rule simply: Anyone breaking the truce would find himself barred from trading with him.

Alice returned Seraphine's gaze with a warm smile. *Is that a hint of madness in your eyes, or are you just pretending?* Seraphine never knew.

After a few minutes, Nix returned with a palm-sized data reader. Sliding the crystal into its cradle, she tapped several buttons and murmured something in her native tongue.

While they were waiting, Seraphine heard Alice singing to herself. It was an ancient nursery rhyme:

"The sheep's in the meadow, the cow's in the corn;

"But where is the boy who looks after the sheep?

"He's under a haystack, fast asleep."

Seraphine glanced over the quarterdeck, her eyes landing on Viktor. He was by the cathedral at the fore of the starship, head down, standing still like a forgotten shadow. The collar around his neck gleamed in the soft light. She noticed the vacant, dull look in his eyes as he shuffled along, barely noticed by the crew.

A quiet breath escaped her. There was nothing she could do here.

The universe is a game, Viktor. I'm just playing to win.

Her mind lingered on him, still scheming.

A soft hum bloomed, and a moment later, the hologram of a star chart flickered into view. Lines of light traced out a path, showing the way to a distant star. Then, a luminous world appeared, rotating slowly. It was a sphere of blue oceans and green continents, unmarred and untouched.

Nix's eyes widened. "It's beautiful."

Alice smiled. "So, it isn't a weapon after all."

Seraphine's breath caught. "It's the location of an Eden planet."

Shtol crossed his arms. "What is an Eden planet?"

Seraphine closed her eyes. A breeze passed over the deck, cool and fragrant with salt. She murmured aloud, "An Eden planet is a pure, clean world, uninhabited. Ready for colonization without alien entanglements. It's a term we used in the scout service for a mythical world we could never find."

When she opened her eyes, Ingli was staring at her in silent thanks.

Seraphine returned the thought with a nod.

Alice whistled low. "A whole new world to play with. I wonder if it'd make a good base for my new starship?"

The felinoid sauntered over and sat on the deck, watching the pretty hologram spin in the air above their heads. For a moment, Seraphine thought he might take a swipe at it with a paw. She shook her head just as he spoke. "It's a bit out of the way. If we sent a team of robot slaves, they could build a city for us."

Seraphine turned to the girl. "What do you want to do with your world, Ingli?"

A smile rose, quiet and bright, like sunlight cresting a new world

* * *

Puffy clouds drifted overhead, throwing shadows across the beach. The cafe overlooked the ocean over the wind-rippled harbor of New Kingston, Eleutheria. Seabirds wheeled above the surf, their cries sharp in the breeze. Seraphine and William sat in the sunshine, sharing a bottle of champagne.

"Leopold Voss said we're out of Archon bombs, did he?" asked

William.

"Yes," she said. "So its the end of an age. A time when humanity decided to turn the galaxy into a graveyard. Into it we buried all of our reason and compassion and we covered it up with our hate."

"Oh, we still have hate." William refilled their glasses. "What's irritating is that you only brought me back a few trifles from Archon."

They drank. The star 783 Gliese glittered off the water.

Alice's crew had plundered loot from Archon, but Seraphine's crew had liberated it from *The Queen of Diamonds* when they had rescued Alice's crew. Seraphine wondered if it was wise to exploit the technology of the ancients. Her thoughts drifted to Christian Thiessen, now a prisoner of the 9th Legion.

Nearby, an outdoor holo-viewer broadcast a news report. Footage played of the fight between William and the assassins—spliced to look like Seraphine had attacked him. It ended with a wanted poster, her face displayed above a sizable bounty.

William chuckled. "They're saying that you tried to kill me," he said. "A rogue pirate who tried to assassinate a praefect."

Seraphine's lips twisted into a smile that didn't reach her eyes. "Ah, I do love a good story," she mused. "I've been declared an enemy of the Imperium. All good citizens are bound to do me harm, if they can."

William grinned, his eyes gleaming with amusement. "Yes, it makes it legal for anyone to kill you."

Everyone loves a good game.

She drank down the rest of her champagne. "Why didn't you tell them the truth?"

William sipped his. His voice was calm, almost amused. "Follow the nature of the universe. Ride the current without trying to impose your will upon it and you will handle life much better."

"You won't let me retire, will you?"

He set his glass down with a soft clink, his smile sharp. "I still have need of you."

She crossed her arms. "Perhaps I have other plans."

"Work for me, Seraphine, or I will turn you in."

You really think you can?

The wind teased her hair, but her eyes stayed hard on the horizon.

*   *   *

On the quarterdeck of the *Lethe*, Seraphine and her crew prepared to take off. She glanced at them. "Now that this black spot is over with, where shall we go?"

Gisele leaned back in her chair, her voice casual but sharp. "Captain, no intention to take offense, but aren't you wanted by the authorities?"

"Yes, there's that." Seraphine paused, her expression thoughtful for a moment, as if mulling over the question. A mischievous glint sparkled in her eyes before she flashed a grin. "I'm just getting started."

Sebastian leaned forward. "Shall we go hunting, captain?"

"Indeed, we shall." Seraphine raised her arms wide. "Starward ho!"

The *Lethe* blasted off the planet and sailed away into the stars.

THE END

MARK O'BANNON
Biography

Mark O'Bannon is an American novelist, screenwriter, and game designer best known as the author of the science fiction series *Imperium* and for three fantasy series: *Whiskers, Aia the Barbarian,* and *Shadows and Dreams.*

O'Bannon is the CEO of Shadowstar Games, which publishes the Interactive Storytelling Game (a Pen & Paper Role Playing Game), "Fantasy Imperium."

O'Bannon is an advocate of Self-Publishing and teaches workshops to aspiring authors on how to publish, market and promote their work.

Born in San Diego, California, O'Bannon is the grandson of the famous aviation pioneer, Reuben H. Fleet (who acquired the Wright Brother's airplane company Dayton-Wright along with Gallaudet Aircraft and formed Consolidated Aircraft, the makers of the famous B-24 Liberator bombers and the PB-Y Catalina flying boats from WWII).

O'Bannon is a registered Libertarian and runs a non-profit, Mapping Freedom, which teaches Free World Theory (FWT), an exploration of the freedoms protected by the U.S. Constitution, and new scientific discoveries of freedom, coercion, property, slavery and intellectual property.